Running into a Brick Wall

A Romantic RV Adventure

Books by Jacqueline DeGroot

Climax
The Secret of the Kindred Spirit
What Dreams Are Made Of
Barefoot Beaches
For the Love of Amanda
Shipwrecked at Sunset
Worth Any Price
Father Steve's Dilemma
The Widows of Sea Trail—Book One
Catalina of Live Oaks
The Widows of Sea Trail—Book Two
Tessa of Crooked Gulley
The Widows of Sea Trail—Book Three
Vivienne of Sugar Sands
Running into Temptation
with Peggy Grich
Running up the Score
with Peggy Grich
Running into a Brick Wall
with Peggy Grich
Tales of the Silver Coast—*A Secret History of*
Brunswick County
with Miller Pope
Sunset Beach—*A History*
with Miller Pope

Running into a Brick Wall

A Romantic RV Adventure

by
Jacqueline DeGroot
with
Peggy Grich

©2011 by Jacqueline DeGroot

Published by American Imaging
Cover design: Miller Pope
Format and packaging: Peggy Grich

Printed in the United States of America

First Edition 2011

ISBN 978-1-4507-7806-0

This book is a work of fiction. All characters in this book have no existence outside the imagination of the author and have no relation whatsoever to anyone bearing the same name or names.

Dedicated to the millions of people who have embraced a lifestyle that allows them to live and travel on their own terms.

You deserve an adventure written around your experiences. Although RVing isn't always easy, your home on wheels, no matter the size, is truly the best of all worlds.

There's something about giving in to a sense of wanderlust that is appealing and basic in all of us..

Acknowledgments

Thank you to my proofreaders:

Deb Coyte
Bill DeGroot
Peggy Grich
Pam McNeel
Martha Murphy

Miller Pope for the wonderful cover depicting my beloved Dolphin.

Peggy Grich for editing, formatting, and packaging the final manuscript—and helping to sell the books. What an amazing partner, and friend, she and her husband Jim are greatly missed.

And for my family for being so supportive of a writing career that keeps me very active and often distracted.

Running into a Brick Wall

A Romantic RV Adventure

Chapter One

I came down the side of the mountain and marveled at the town spread out below me. It looked so peaceful with each house and building placed in neat little rows. The tallest structure was easily the church; its steeple stark white against the backdrop of the blue-green mountains. The town was named Hillvalley, which I thought was very odd—how can a place be both a hill and a valley? Then I drove around another curve and I got my answer. I was coming down a hill, and the little town completely filled the valley floor. I was coming from the hill to the valley—it seemed appropriately named now. Perfect, in fact.

As I meandered down, careful of the narrow switchbacks and the jutting rocky-sided mountain, I feared for my wide RV. The spikes of rock ledges seemed awfully close as I navigated the curves. I didn't want to get too near to the opposite edge of the road either. The steep drop-offs looked even closer to my tires in a vehicle of this size. Of all the places I expected to find Brick, this was definitely not it—there was absolutely nothing metropolitan here. It did not smack me in the face as having his type of crime. This area was all about farming and mining. And unless I missed my guess, hunters and moonshine were no strangers here. When Brick said come meet me in the hills of

Kentucky, I'd had no idea how back woodsy the area would be. This was quaint, although it seemed to my mind, an unlikely place for the type of criminal Brick normally chased.

It took another hour to maneuver my home, a.k.a. my National RV Dolphin, all the way down the mountain and to find the tiny slate-shingled, pewter gray building Brick had described. With its nondescript front, this was the most unobtrusive police station I had ever seen. I wasn't even sure it was a police station until I stepped inside.

A handful of men where milling around four desks piled high with stacks of dusty files on the corners. All had badges on their hips and guns in shoulder holsters. They looked up when I opened the door and then stared at me as if they'd never seen a woman before. A somber mood pervaded, I couldn't say why I thought that, I just felt it. I asked for Brick Tyler and was shown to a hallway with several doors. A stoop-shouldered gentleman with an old-fashioned Fedora-styled hat that he held respectfully in his hand, nodded and said, "Knock on the door at the end of the hall there, they's watching sumpin' vulgar and vile. Give 'em a chance to shut it off."

Brick had called and asked me to take a detour to meet him here. At the time I had no idea what he wanted, but I knew from his tone that there was something gnawing at him from the inside. It was as if he was choking on anger when he asked me to meet him. Initially I thought his phone call might have something to do with his sister who had been missing for several years. From his tone, it sounded like they might have found her— and not in a good way. But he assured me that wasn't the case.

He told me this was about another little girl, but said he just couldn't talk about it yet. From the catch and rasp of his voice I knew this wasn't going to be good. But if he thought I could help with whatever he was so angry over, I knew I had to try. He'd certainly come to my rescue, and more than once. Just recently, in Virginia when my estranged husband was holding me hostage, he had risked his life and saved me. I could do no less for him. But how could I possibly help him? He was big, strong—fearless. I was petite, fragile and just on the cusp of getting my feisty back.

I am Jenny, a woman on the run from a very wicked soon-to-be ex-husband. Three months ago I left my overbearing, jealous, possessive, son-of-a-bitch husband after I had finally built up enough courage and enough cash to make what I thought was the perfect escape—a life on the road in a motorhome.

But I had seriously underestimated my husband and he found me. The belly button piercing he had insisted on installing several years before held some type of transmitter and he tracked me down and tried to drag me back home. I evaded him several times but managed to fall into a trap he set, and for ten long days I was forced to be his sex slave again. He fancied himself to be a dominant and since he had not been able to coerce me into playing his submissive voluntarily, he broke all the rules for BDSM and forced me.

Then Brick and his team found me. Brick is an agent for the North Carolina Bureau of Investigation; he specializes in crimes against children. When he saw what Jared had done to me, he beat him bloody and senseless. I spent a week in the hospital recovering from the abuse I'd been subjected to. Nothing serious enough to require surgery and nothing I wouldn't recover from, but my doctor wanted to keep me isolated from both law enforcement and the media. I didn't need the questions, the attention, or the stress. And as I had no place to stay . . . the hospital room became my hotel room until I was back on my feet. Jared could afford it and I made sure he was billed for everything.

I hadn't seen Brick since being released. I hadn't wanted to. I hadn't wanted to see anyone. I just wanted to crawl into a hole and hide. And then, after reuniting with my cell phone, I found I'd had a call from Randy, a fellow camper I'd met in Las Cruces, New Mexico.

His message had been short and sweet, "One of my guys

on the set-up crew knows this Robert Byrnes guy you're looking for. So give me a call when you get a chance and for heaven's sake make it during the day. We've talked, and Charlotte's getting better, but I'm still on a very short leash and you're way too pretty by far for her to be comfortable with me talkin' to you."

I'd returned his call and set plans in motion to be in Redmond, Oregon in three weeks when The Rally was there. I was going to make Brick very happy. I was going to find his baby sister who was stolen by a husband and wife team four years ago. Of course, I wasn't going to tell him about it, yet—he'd had too many leads and false tips go awry to get him all churned up just to end up disappointed again. I was going to go undercover on my own and find her. I could envision Brick's face when I placed her in his loving arms. It would be a life-changing event—for both of us.

But meanwhile, by special request, I was here in this little burg and very curious as to what Brick wanted with me. I knocked, waited a few seconds, and then opened the door.

Chapter Two

Brick was hunched over a desk watching a small TV—his head cupped in his hand, his voice low and hoarse as he talked to a man seated on his right. He turned to face the door when it opened and saw me, then jumped up and rushed over. I was clasped tight to his chest and the breath was hugged out of me. It felt wonderful to be held by him, but I knew his grip would be deadly if I didn't get him to back off, and soon. He began murmuring in my ear, "Jenny, Jenny, Jenny," as if he couldn't get enough of saying my name. Then after a slight hesitation, he whispered, "You are still using Jenny, aren't you?" In an effort to outrun my husband I had changed my name twice, but I really liked Jenny, and with Jared in jail it didn't seem necessary to change my name again.

I managed to nod despite him gripping my head hard to his chest. His big hand was comforting and I loved the fresh linen smell of his dress shirt, but I couldn't seem to get a full breath.

"Uh, hi. Not so tight, Brick. I can't breathe."

"Oh sorry, I'm just happy to see you. You can't know how pleased I am that you came."

I smiled up at him and saw a haggard face, haunted eyes,

5

and a feral light I'd seen once before—the first time he'd taken on Jared, when he'd wanted to kill him and I hadn't let him.

"What's the matter?" I asked as I put my hand on his cheek. I felt the stubble of a beard in full bloom. "You don't look as though you've slept in a week."

"I haven't. Just the kind of sleep that comes with nightmares." He pointed to the man still sitting in the chair. "This is my boss, Agent Joe Rydell. We're watching a video of a bust gone bad; my bust, and I'm the one who blew it. Big time. I need you to watch it with me. It's going to be hard for you to watch, but you need to if you're going to be onboard with helping us out. I told Joe you had some law enforcement training, that you were a campus policeman your junior and senior year at UVA so he agreed we could use you if you think you're up to it. Here, have a seat; we might as well get this over with. It's bad, Jen. Really bad. I fucked up."

His hands left my waist and raked through his hair leaving thick segments in ridges. "I lost my cool. I lost all control." His eyes met mine and I saw the despair, then he turned and sat back in the chair he'd just jumped up from. I was pulled into the seat beside him and the video monitor was moved back.

"There's no signal for my wireless here so we have to use this old set up. It's grainy, but you'll have no trouble seeing what's going on."

I watched as he rewound the tape on the ancient VCR. From the sure action of his fingers on the keys I knew that he'd been watching it over and over again, probably all morning from the way he was in tune with the machine. It seemed he knew exactly when to stop rewinding. He pressed play and I turned my attention to the screen. It was dim, but I saw the outline of a bed and then a little girl propped at the head of it. Her clothing was askew and it looked as if her tiny white bra straps were pulled off her shoulders. One small breast was pulled up and over a cup. A disembodied voice broke the silence, a man's gravely voice.

"Hi Susie. You've been such a good girl today, doing

everything your Uncle John said to do, such a good little girl you are. It's my turn to play with your sweet little body. Your teeny little breasts and your rosy little nipples are so sexy. They look so pretty poking out of your cute training bra, just begging for attention. I'm going to hold you and touch you, make you feel good, so good. I promise not to hurt you. Just let me touch you, okay?"

The girl, who was still holding on to her baby fat as she entered puberty, appeared to be heavily drugged, her eyes blank in her chubby face as she gave what could be assumed was a muttered assent and a vague nod.

"Good girl, I'm so glad it's finally my turn. So many men got to sample you first, to try you out with their fingers so they could decide. But don't worry, no one will be allowed to put their penis inside you until I say they can." His hand caressed her breast, kneading it roughly. "Don't worry, because I'm beginning to think you might be the one I choose to keep. Would you like that, being my girlfriend?"

Another blank look and another tiny drop of her head.

The man, short with a huge paunch, sat on the bed beside the young girl, depressing the mattress considerably. The fingers of one hand were pinching and pulling on the tiny budded nipple that poked over the cup of the white cotton bra while with his other hand he unzipped his zipper. The girl's eyes went wide with fear when his penis popped through the opening. She sobbed as he gripped her hand and brought it to him.

Seconds later, undercover officers burst into the room and half naked men, each holding a doped up girl in their lap, jumped up and scattered. The man who had been fondling Susie gave a great roar and charged the last officer coming through the door. The screen went haywire with blurry images before going black.

Brick stopped the tape. I watched as his finger automatically hit the rewind button. What was it that made us rerun the worst moments of our lives over and over again, hoping for a different ending? I sat there waiting for him to speak. I had absolutely no idea what I could say to make it better or make it go away. I knew this kind of thing happened, but I had never been witness to it. Watching it was far worse than I thought it could possibly be.

Finally, he spoke, "I had to stop it right there. I couldn't watch that pervert touch her like that any longer. And because of it, he got away. I knew we weren't ready to go in. The man you saw there, John Howard, he ran like a line backer into one of my guys, knocked him on his ass, crushed a few ribs, and then he made off on an ATV he'd had hidden behind the motel. We gave chase, but he knew the surrounding woods—Christ this was his fucking hometown at one time. Anyway, we lost him. And it's all my fault. Mine. He's gonna get a chance at other girls now, because of me!"

I could see the anguish in his eyes. It pained me to see him hurting so badly. I didn't know what to say, so I said nothing, just stared at the man I was coming to love as he fell to pieces. Finally our eyes met, his bloodshot and wounded, mine filled with tears of compassion. He took a deep breath and said, "And that's where you come in, if you want to."

"Oh, I want to. I definitely want to. What kind of a man does that to such a young girl? I want to do anything I can to help out."

"We have an agent on loan from Vermont. She's twenty-four, but dressed like a schoolgirl you'd swear she was no more than fourteen. She's agreed to go undercover so we can get this guy and shut him down for good. We've been after him for months now, but he always manages to allude us, just like he did yesterday. This time, we're determined to get him or die trying. We figure he's responsible for kidnapping and drugging thirty-six little girls, ages ten to sixteen. He likes them young and so do the men he arranges to sell them to. Eight still haven't been recovered."

"Ohhh God. How awful!" It made my stomach clench, just the thought of what these girls were going through. I thought I might be sick but I didn't want to show it. I wanted to be strong for Brick. I dug in my purse for a cough drop and sucked on it while Brick paced.

"Yeah. So if you agree to help out, we'd really appreciate it."

"Don't worry, I'm on board. Just what do you need me to do?"

"Dress down, slum yourself up a bit and pretend to be this agent's neglectful, self-serving mother."

"Her mother!" *Boy that wasn't very flattering.* Then I did some fast addition in my head. Fourteen, could have had her at sixteen, okay being taken for thirty wasn't all that bad. I was twenty-eight after all. "Okay, I suppose I could do that, no problem."

He flashed me a big grin and it was worth the six hundred-mile detour just to see that bright, sexy smile plastered on his ruggedly handsome face again. With his curving sensuous lips and straight white teeth, I doubted any woman could say no to him, least of all me. I was all but acknowledging the inevitability of the fact that I was falling in love with him. Okay, okay, so darned near all the way into that free-fall that I doubted anything could change the outcome at this point. But this was not the time to tell him that.

"Our informant says John Howard never misses his momma's birthday, so he'll be in Knoxville two days from now to see her blow out her birthday candles, and soon after, he'll be looking for a new victim to warm his bed. Hopefully that'll be enough time to turn you into a scag who has no qualms about whoring her daughter for drug money."

"When you say scag, you don't mean cutting my hair, knocking out teeth, or messing with my eyebrows, do you?"

He came over to stand in front of me and softly caressed my check, then his fingers moved to the back of my neck and he stroked me there. I felt his heat and my skin responded with that telltale tingle that had me fighting to keep my hands to myself.

"No, we won't do anything permanent. A few henna tattoos, a mousy hair rinse with some goop to make your beautiful hair look dry, chipped nail polish on chewed off nails, and tons of gaudy make-up should do the trick."

"Good, I'd hate to *remain* scaggy after this is all over."

"Mmm," he said as he looked me over, "I can't wait to see you skanked out a bit." He leaned in and put his forehead to mine and whispered so no one else in the room could hear, "I sure wish I was going to be the one to pick out your slutty outfit. I'd love to see you in fishnets with huge holes in them, and a plunging see-through blouse over a tawdry mini-skirt."

"See-through!" I gasped, a bit louder than I'd intended. He put his fingertips to my lips. His boss was sitting at the table watching our little reunion and just outside the door was a bustling police station.

"Just joking. I don't want anyone, least of all this perv seeing you topless."

I looked into his face, my own creased with worry. "Speaking of . . . what have all your friends been saying . . . uh, on that score?" I'd had the unfortunate experience of being rescued in my all-together a few weeks earlier, but despite Brick's efforts to shield me, his whole team had had an eyeful of my 38Cs. I still flushed red whenever I thought about it.

"We don't talk about it. But if anyone did, there's hardly anything they could say, except how lucky I am that you're my girl."

"Am I your girl?"

His boss got up and left the room, mumbling something about a meeting in ten minutes.

Chapter Three

"Of course you're my girl. I would hope by now that you'd have no doubt about that. I mean, sure, after all we've been through it's been tough to have a normal romance, but we'll get there. After this is all wrapped up, I think you and I need to take some time, get to know each other . . . check and see if this is chemistry we're feeling or something deeper."

"What are you opting for?"

"Something deeper, not so transient."

"White picket fence," I chided. It was something he had mentioned while I was in the hospital, but I was fairly certain he had forgotten.

He smiled at me and chucked my chin. "I know I offered, but I just can't picture you as the white picket fence type. I saw your house, remember? You're more the castle with the moat type."

"Actually, I'm pretty happy with my Dolphin."

"Speaking of which, your driving skills must have really improved for you to have made it down into this valley."

"Took my time and held my breath all the way down."

He chuckled and then his eyes met mine. There was a spark of sadness in them that I had never truly seen disappear.

"Thank you for coming."

"How could I not?" He was so handsome even disheveled, so tall, and right now so melancholy it actually hurt my chest to see it.

"Hey, you don't have to do this. We can get someone else."

"That would take time you don't have. Sounds like this is all coming down pretty quickly."

"It is. But we could fly someone in."

"Not necessary. I'm honored. And just a bit curious."

"About what?"

"Playing the role, getting trashed-up so to speak. Seeing if I can put a smile back on your face when you get this guy."

His fingers cupped my chin and he bent to brush the softest, most tender kiss I've ever had across my lips. It spoke volumes. I could feel the need as well as a fierce undertow of possessiveness as he deepened the kiss and moved his lips over mine. Then his large hand slid up my jaw and wrapped around my head bringing me closer. His mouth captured mine and claimed it. There was nowhere his tongue didn't delve; nowhere our lips didn't mesh. The only thing that kept me from sinking deeper into the abyss was the sound of his boss clearing his throat behind us.

Brick ended the kiss, but not abruptly, despite the audience, he still let his lips linger, his tongue taste, before pulling back. His hand fell to my waist where he gripped it before turning me and leading me through the door.

Until then I hadn't known I was to be a part of the meeting, but it soon became apparent that I was considered part of the team and had to be included so I could thoroughly understand my role.

Soon, the makeshift office they were using would be dismantled and moved to Kentucky, along with me—the new and not-so-proud mother of a teenage girl who was going to surprise this John Howard by kicking his ass.

As soon as we sat at the improvised conference table consisting of two folding tables pushed together, Brick's boss stood and paced the perimeter of the room. "This man is fully bankrolled by his mama, he dotes on her and she dotes on him, but despite what he says or how he acts in public, his main focus in life is to always please his mama. It's not clear to what extent she condones his pedophilic lifestyle, but the pattern she's shown all his life is to deny him nothing. Absolutely nothing. It's rumored she secured two young teenaged girls for him as a birthday present when he was fifteen. Paid them five hundred each to make sure he woke up a happy little man. He is her only child, and while he left her to manage her huge hog farm all on her own, she doesn't seem to hold that against him . . . so long as he visits regularly. The pattern we've mapped out seems to include all major holidays, her birthday and his, with occasional surprise visits we suspect are for allowance issues. As I said she holds the purse strings. Of course, she does all the work, so I'm not thinking he minds her being in charge all that much.

"In two days she's putting on a big to do in a bar in her hometown to celebrate her birthday, the whole town has been invited and there's talk she would like a grandchild—soon. Junior, always obliging, as I said, will probably be pressured to pick a local woman and settle down. But so far, his tastes don't run to the motherly type. He seems to draw the line at seventeen-year olds. Although the odds are fairly high he's impregnated at least one of his victims at one time or another, mama's probably looking for progeny to cuddle and spoil like her son. And of course, there's the farm—down the road she's going to want to retire. Sonny boy either has no desire or no talent for running an enterprise that's put the town on the map."

"How old is mama?" Brick asked.

"Fifty-two."

"And no husband?"

"Been out of the picture for fourteen years. She divorced

him when she found him in the barn with her sister. The sister hasn't been seen since then, maybe she went with him, maybe she didn't—at least that's the way she's always answered the question concerning her whereabouts."

"So what time's the party, and are we all going to just saunter into town and belly up to the bar?"

"The party is on the 5th, starts at sundown, and everyone's invited. A stranger is going to be suspect though, so we'll keep it to a minimum. Jenny, you'll be there with your daughter *Vanessa*, your car will break down just outside town. Brick and Jed, you'll be two truckers on the road. The rest of us will be inside the back of the truck monitoring everything *and* calling the shots. He said this last part while giving Brick a stern look. We will *not* jump the gun this time. As everyone has watched that tape over and over again, I'm sure you all realize that we do not have enough evidence to put this man away. We only have his voice, and him from the back. This time we're going to have everything nailed down. So nailed down that good ol' mama is going to have to visit her son in jail for her next birthday. Got that?"

Everyone nodded or murmured their assent and then chairs scraped on the wooden floor as the meeting came to a close. Brick's boss motioned for both of them to join him at the head of the table where he was still pacing.

"Jenny, your *daughter* will be here this evening, along with the agent who's going to ugly you up a bit. You two can bunk together over at the B & B on Dawson, the rest of us will be in the old Army barracks on Maplewood. We'll leave at six a.m., plenty of time to get there and roll into town for Junior's momma's birthday party.

"All you have to do is parade Vanessa around a bit, indicate she's more trouble than she's worth and that for two cents you'd ditch her right then and there. Act a bit shaky like you need a fix and then negotiate whatever he offers—then take the money and run. When he spirits Vanessa away we'll be right there, eyes and ears recording. When he makes his move, this time we'll have him surrounded."

He looked her in the eye, trying to gauge her, to sense her spirit or her gumption. "Got it? Any problems with any of that?"

"I've got it. Sounds easy enough. Where do I go when I get back in my car and leave?"

"We'll be set up at a travel park in the next town over, that's where we'll leave the RVs—yours, Brick's, and the rest of the team's. Just head back there and wait for us. It'll take a while because we'll have to hand him off to Federal marshals before we can join you. No way are we leaving him anywhere where his mama can get to him. Why don't you go get something to eat and rest up, we'll come get you when Vanessa gets here."

I looked up at Brick and saw the thoughtful expression on his face. I knew he was already planning contingencies, seeing everything happening and reacting to it all in his mind. I could tell he was in no mood to baby-sit me for the next few hours.

"Sure. I'll just go back to my RV and have a snack. Then I'll take a nap. You know where to find me."

Brick came out of his reverie long enough to walk me back to the RV I'd left parked at the far end of the parking lot. I unlocked the door and then he turned me back to him as I was about to go up the steps.

"I have to go check all the electronics, make sure there are no glitches. You look tired. Grab some soup or a sandwich and then get some rest. I'll come check on you after I'm done." His hands fell from my shoulders to my arms and then to my wrists.

He brought them to his lips and kissed each one. I felt the warmth seep all the way down into my fur-lined Uggs. He leaned in and kissed my forehead. "Thank you," he whispered, and then turned and left.

I watched his tall frame move away, his shoulders slightly hunched as he stared at the ground and ate up the distance with his long, lean legs. On the outside he was a force to be reckoned with. But on the inside, he was fragile. He was doubting himself and he was still bashing his head against the wall of disgrace and humiliation. I could feel how all this was affecting him. I could sense his despair. But there was nothing I could do about it. At least not until tomorrow when I would sashay into the bar, crash Junior's momma's birthday party, and sell him my make-believe daughter for his perverse sexual needs. Then Brick could avenge himself. He would time it right this time and put that bastard away where he couldn't hurt little girls anymore.

As I turned and climbed the steps into my RV, I touched my lips and remembered Brick's all-consuming kiss, full of need and desire, laced with the possessiveness of a man who knew what he wanted but careful enough to make sure his woman had the same needs and wants. It was how every girl, every woman, deserved to be kissed—her innocence taken with awe and respect, not inconsequentially and with force.

Chapter Four

I was sleeping like the dead, all bundled up, knees to my chest, face into my pillow when I sensed I wasn't alone anymore. I slowly opened my eyes and assessed that feeling. I was sure there was a distinct reason for it. Then I smiled. Brick's big, splayed hand was on my butt, not kneading or caressing, but just holding and letting his warmth seep into the rounded cheek that I had hiked up in the air.

Slowly I turned and opened my eyes to the dim interior of my bedroom. I almost always kept the blinds drawn back here but I could still tell that it was late in the afternoon; the light seeping between the cracks had lost its shimmer and was morbid with shadows. When I managed to get fully turned so I could see his sleeping form, my world lit again. He was magnificent in repose. This man who allowed me to see him when he was so vulnerable, so wounded by failure.

His dark brows were relaxed, there were no frown lines marring his smooth forehead—his cheeks, far from being smooth shaven had their own dark shadows blooming on them. His jaw was taut leading down to a chiseled chin with the slightest hint of a dent. He looked latently dangerous, a powerful Titan. But it was his lips that drew me. Partially open and emitting the softest puffs of air, they were firm and welcoming, a lovely shade of rose that I wanted to taste. I leaned in and the scent of him encased me, spiking something visceral within me. His lips were warm under mine, firm, yet welcoming. I couldn't get enough. My lips plucked at his bottom lip, tasting, exploring the texture, and drinking in the sensation of knowing I was being intimate with the most sensual pair of lips on earth. I heard him moan, long and low and then I was on my back and he was covering me with his body, his jean-clad knee insinuating itself between my legs.

Tongues are amazing things. They can lick, soothe, feather, flicker, and together with lips they can suck, stroke, caress and nip tauntingly. His did all that and more, drinking me hungrily as if he couldn't get enough of the flavor, of the taste that now was essentially us. Deep throaty groans accompanied rasping forays and searching plunges, until I couldn't tell which ones were his and which ones came from me. When his hand slid down my cheek to my throat and then to my breast, I had no trouble telling which groan was mine. His were deep and throaty—full of appreciation, mine were low and keening as my body arched and I tried to feed my breast to his palm . . . and then to his mouth. Still I needed more. Much more. I was almost in pain from the yearning, the intense desire burning through me, lighting little fires everywhere. *Please, please*, my mind screamed, *take off my shirt. For the love of God, touch me there—naked . . . please.*

He finally did. My long-sleeved tee was stripped off, my bra unclasped and my breasts freed, ready to be lavished. His knee slid up the sheet, wedged high between my thighs and pressed against me over and over again in a knowing, male-inspired rhythm. I came, shuddering uncontrollably long before either of us expected it. He drew me to him, holding me tight and tucking his face into my neck. He murmured soothing phrases I could only catch a word or two of—*lovely, sweet, so sexy, primed were you? Love how you taste, want you badly—*

crooning sounds that made me realize we weren't going any further right now. *Why not?*

I wiggled my hand down between our bodies and gripped him. He jerked and pushed into my palm letting me feel how much he wanted me. He was long and hard, it was at least to my mind, impossible to believe he wasn't going to do something about this. I was game for any scenario. Any place, any way, however he wanted me—I was there to comply. My lust meter was pegged; I was in the red zone. It had been a long time since I wanted a man inside me. I had *needed* one many times but had found alternatives that required a little help from Duracell.

"No," he whispered against my ear. "No."

"Yes," I whispered back. "Yes."

"You deserve better."

I pushed him back so I could see his face. "What does that mean?" I asked, clearly confused.

"You deserve better. I'm such a fuck-up."

I pushed hard against his chest, sending him over onto his side. "You are not going to tell me that because of this . . . this . . . error in judgment on your part, that you are not worthy of me! I am the one not worthy of you. You are amazing—a wonderful, caring man. You are not a fuck-up. And one way or another, I am going to have you. Right now."

Using both hands I undid his jeans and began wrestling them open. His hands joined mine as he tried to keep me from releasing him. But I was driven. I wanted his cock. In my hand, in my pussy, in my mouth—right now it didn't really matter where. I wanted to give him pleasure. I wanted to love him. I wanted to show him that *I* didn't deserve *him*. And the best way to do that, I reasoned, was to be submissive—to take him inside my mouth and love him, soothe his hurts, lave his bruised pride. If Brick could be the one to benefit from the long hours Jared had spent tutoring me in the art of fellatio, that would please me very much. He fought me as I angled myself down onto the bed, as I turned my face into his crotch. But he stopped fighting the instant I took him into my mouth. The struggle was over. He succumbed as I greedily sucked and licked his penis. I curled into him, and like a baby with a pacifier; I would not let him go.

A long sigh escaped, then a deep throaty groan, then his hand cupped my head and he showed me the rhythm he desired. I marveled at how steel encased in flesh could feel so silky in my hand and feel so warm in my mouth. It had been years since I had found any satisfaction in pleasing a man this way. His total fulfillment was my only goal but a sixth sense told me he would never allow himself to come in my mouth. I knew I had another battle drawing near when he began to jerk and sob my name with distress. But I held on despite his efforts to buck me off and when he came I sucked his slick cum down my throat as it spewed from him, enjoying every single shudder that told me he had given me complete control. Finally. I continued to lick and suck until he went flaccid in my mouth. He caressed individual locks of my hair in long sensuous strokes until his hand went limp and I heard his even breaths. He was spent, and delightfully so.

I turned myself around on the bed, wrapped my arms around him, and covered us with the comforter. An hour later a knock at the door woke us and we were told Vanessa had arrived. It was show time. Time to get to know my daughter, and then time to get the show on the road. And soon it would be time to put the filthy bastard who was messing with little girls, and now with my man's self esteem, in a big ol' federal prison.

We crawled out on opposite sides of the bed but before I could round the bottom of the bed he grabbed me by the wrist and walked me over to a chair in the living area. Then pulled me into his lap. "You asked if you were my girlfriend. Who else's would you be? I can't think of anybody else who would put up with you."

He kissed me lightly on the lips, grazing softly to lick at both corners. "You're a lot of trouble . . . damned nuisance at times," he murmured as he ran the tip of his tongue along the seam of my lower lip. "More trouble than you're worth, that's for sure . . ." he muttered as his hands came up to frame my face and his tongue delved deep inside to capture mine. His low groan of pleasure as I slipped my tongue alongside his and kissed him back sent heat through me. I was hungry for this man, ravished in fact. Desire heated my skin, flashed through my veins and sent wild images flickering like porn on a Nickelodeon on the backside of my eyelids—images of him naked on top of me, plunging his hard penis into me as I arched to receive it and take it as deep as I could; him, holding my knees spread wide as his head dipped; him taking me from the back with his hands caressing my breasts; him, doing everything man was made to do with and to a woman.

If it hadn't been for people yelling back and forth on the other side of the door, I believe I would have unzipped him right there and made him put that hard ridge inside me so I could ride him like a cowgirl while he sat in that chair.

But it wasn't time for that yet. And I think we both knew it. When we finally did the deed, I wanted him to be all mine, body and soul. And right now his soul was tied up in this mess, and his thoughts were nowhere near being solely on me. We had to do this thing first. We had to find this guy, lure him in and take him down, and then, maybe then, I would tell him I'd fallen off the cliff without a parachute.

Chapter Five

Vanessa, while appearing very young, was smart, experienced, and inspired confidence. She was cheerful and helpful and made my "transformation" easy and fun. Juanita, the agent that had accompanied her, brought a chest full of makeup and wigs and trunks filled with all manner of clothing. Knowing I was to be a down-on-her luck single mother who tended toward the trashy side, I was still surprised at the final result.

My pristine pearly whites were now tinged yellow (I was assured that the stain was temporary) and a silver cap was visible when I smiled. Crowfeet had been etched with brown fine-line markers around my eyes and gray shadows were created to make me look weary. Fine lines had been added around my mouth and dark red lipstick had been applied purposefully so that it bled and created hard, coarse lips. Some concoction Juanita had come up with made my eyes tear and gave me blood-shot eyes in twenty seconds. Then my body was squeezed into too-tight jeans creating the effect of dreaded muffin-tops over my hips, which disgustingly enough were to be very apparent as the jeans were low slung and the skinny-strapped, madras-styled baby-doll top was inches from meeting the waistband. Normally I wouldn't mind my midriff being so exposed, but this was hard, displaying such a distracting and unflattering area, flaunting the fact that I was not only tacky but on the verge of being fat and lazy, I didn't like it one bit. An underwire push-up bra worked on creating the impression that if I could only manage to get my neck down low enough, I could suck my own nipples. Looking in the mirror, I had never seen my breasts higher on my chest or my cleavage deeper. It bordered on obscene.

Next, my hair was colored using an ugly brunette rinse, and then purple and burnt red highlights were added. The whole mess was teased to high heaven and left to fall down my back and shoulders. Vaseline was applied to the ends in a willy-nilly way to make it look as if I hadn't washed my hair for quite some time.

The ends of my fingernails and toenails were torn unevenly then painted a vile shade of iridescent orange that I was told to work on chipping off when I felt nervous. Vamps that had clearly seen a better day were scuffed up even more before being handed to me to put on. I insisted someone find an anti-fungal spray before putting them on.

I was now the worst imitation I'd ever seen of Olivia Newton-John when she starred in *Grease*. I was shocked when the male agents nodded their approval and winked with undisguised admiration. Brick had to explain the phenomenon most men had of being sexually attracted to truly lusty, low class women. Something about them broadcasting experience along with a devil-may-care attitude and a willingness to try anything if they thought they'd have good time doing it. He added that it coincided with the impression most men had of themselves— that they invariably provided a good time for any woman they deemed to bed.

"But you," he added with a raised brow, "you still manage to come off innocent despite the trappings. I don't know what we can do about that. But darlin', you are sexier than all get out. I'd hump you. I'd hump you against a bar stool if I could get you to bend over it." He leaned in and kissed me on the side of my neck and said, "I guess I like my women on the trashy side."

"Gee. Thanks. Nice to know. Great to hear I'm on your all-time wanted list."

He smiled down at me and put his arm around my waist and drew me close. Then he leaned down and whispered in my ear, "You are wanted. You are needed. Don't ever doubt it. And with or without your cavewoman hair I intend to have you so don't let any of the sleazebags that come on to you bend you over *anything*, you hear?"

Vanessa came out of the bathroom just then and everyone turned to look at the twenty-something turned teenager. She was perfect. Down to her irreverent tube top that hinted at tiny newly formed breasts, to her short paisley mini-skirt and tall white leggings tucked into clunky black patent leather heels. Had the skirt been plaid and the leggings knee-highs, she would have been the classic schoolgirl image popular in porn movies. Braided pigtails completed the image but instead of two, ten braids were gathered together just above her ears and each time she turned they swished back and forth and fanned her youthful face. Yes, she was every pervert's dream girl. Together we made a hell of a team and everyone acknowledged it, even Brick's boss Joe, who I had noticed was slow to praise.

Everyone was given last minute instructions and assignments and then Vanessa and I climbed into the old Dodge clunker that would soon be leaving us stranded by the side of the road—just outside Junior's hometown.

On the hour-long ride Vanessa and I got to know each other, alternating between our roles and our real lives, sizing each other up and deciding we liked what we found in both arenas. As the "mother," I was driving. She was supposedly too young to even have a permit.

"Now, I know it's going to be hard taking the lead as most people tend to gravitate toward the one with the most experience in these things, but *don't*. Remember you're the mother; I'm the daughter. I'm supposed to be subservient to you. Even though I certainly won't be. My job is to act sullen, mad at the world, and at you especially so that when we have our big fight at the party, it can force the separation we need. Then you, being tired of all my shenanigans, can make the rift even bigger so you can capitalize on getting rid of me. Let's role-play until we 'breakdown' to get the emotions right and work out some of the wording."

She and I yelled at each other, throwing accusations back and forth until I got tongue-tied and we ended up laughing ourselves silly. Then I saw her freeze and sit tall. "There's the sign. In three miles you pull over like you're skidding off the road. I'll get out and adjust some things under the hood. Then we wait."

"How long do you think it'll take?" I asked.

"If we stay in the car, forever—if we sit on the trunk, shouldn't be more than half an hour I would think."

Sure enough, half an hour later we were driven into town by a man in his sixties returning from the feed store. We sat on the bench seat of his pick-up and listened to his method of curing tobacco and tried out our roles.

We were deposited at the local garage, which doubled as a gas station and parts store. And while I cried poor and indicated compensation of a different sort as payment if the owner could tow the vehicle in and fix it for us, Vanessa kept up a running banter on how much she hated me and how she couldn't wait until she was sixteen so she could be on her own.

David, the manager of the parts store, offered to drive us to Desperado's, the only place in town where we could get a bite to eat while our car was being checked out, and I thanked God that he was a Christian who only wanted to do a good deed—a gossipy Christian who soon had everyone in the diner/bar/meetin' place up to speed on our predicament.

Sitting at a booth, Vanessa giving me the evil-eye while chomping on fries dipped in mayonnaise, I was approached by two men who offered to buy me a drink. Vanessa kicked me under the table and I found excuses to decline each one. Then with no reason at all, she kicked me again and I saw Junior in all his pudgy splendor ambling over. I recognized him from the photos Brick and Joe had shown me, he was bigger in real life and walked with the swagger that only truly spoiled kids and bullies developed.

"Heard you gals had a bit of car trouble." He was speaking to me, but his eyes were on Vanessa. It was almost comical the way he looked her up and down, his eyes lingering on the portion of her tube top that showed under her flannel over shirt. She reached for her glass and with her thumb swiping in tiny circles, she absentmindedly played with the condensation. I saw the outline of one taut peak poke through the thin knit. From our earlier role-playing I already knew that she was an amazing actress, but darned if I knew how she managed to control that. But Junior sure as hell noticed. He stood straighter and I heard him take in a deep breath. He wanted that barely ripe morsel and honestly, I don't think he cared who knew it because he turned completely from me and slid into the booth beside Vanessa.

"Scooch over sweetheart, let me talk to your mama, maybe I can help you gals out." I had to hand it to the man, he had a nice husky brogue that he countrified. I wondered if he was trying to imitate Hugh Grant or going for an Aussie accent. Whatever it was, it worked—had I been blind, I might have dated the man myself.

I saw his hand move as if caressing her thigh. Then I saw Vanessa shimmy away from him to the other side of the seat.

"Aw, don't be shy. Uncle Jimmy's gonna make everything all better. I can get your car fixed, find you a place to stay tonight, and I'll even buy your dinner." I could smell his overdone cologne mixed with his barnyard body odor, the kind you get when a wet horse blanket is mixed with sweat. I didn't know how Vanessa was handling it sitting next to him.

"Can you make her shut up and leave me alone? 'Cause

I'm sick of her talk, sick of her being spaced-out, and I'm sick of her comin' on to every man in the county who'll give her a cigarette!"

Junior looked over at me and smiled as he whipped a cigarette pack out of his denim jacket and shook it so one stood out. His smile widened into a grin as he reached over and offered it to me. I could all but read his mind. *Here's your cigarette now where's my blowjob?*

I looked over at Vanessa who had a sly grin on her face. *Great.* Now I was going to have to smoke a cigarette. I didn't think I knew how, this was going to be cute. I was going to kill her.

"Uh, thanks," I mumbled as I took the cigarette from the pack he was offering. He reached over with his lighter to light it for me and I put it to my lips. Vanessa gave Junior a hip chuck and said in a whiny voice, "I have to go pee, where's the shit hole in this shit hole?"

Junior looked at her with his eyes wide and pointed to the other side of the bar. Then he eased out of the booth so she could get out and stood staring as her hips did the ba-donk-a-donk all the way across the room. When she disappeared through the door, he took his seat again. I put the cigarette out in her mayonnaise.

"Got a mouth that one does."

"Yeah. She needs someone to teach her a lesson. She's got no respect. For two cents I'd dump her here and leave. She's nothin' but trouble."

He grinned and slapped two pennies on the table. "Well I got two cents."

I smiled with what I thought was evil intent. "I was just jokin'."

"Really?"

"Yeah, about the two cents. She's worth more than that."

"How much more?"

"You offerin'?"

27

"She a virgin?"

"Now how the hell would I know that?" I had already been coached on this one, otherwise I would have been stymied for sure.

"Yeah. Only one way to know for sure, then she's not," he said with a laugh. "But seriously, you need money?"

"Who doesn't? But I need something else, too. You got any pain killers, I got a terrific headache."

"Let's negotiate the girl first, then we can talk about what I can do for your *headache* and whatever else it is that ails you."

"What's the goin' price for a surly fourteen-year-old?" I had been told it was important to establish she was a minor early on.

"I can give you a grand. And I'll fuck the surly right out of her."

"I need more'n that. It's gonna cost five hundred just to get that damn car fixed. Make it twenty-five hundred and you've got a deal. But you've got to keep her, I don't want her back after all your fun and games."

"No problem. I'm in the recycling business." He gave a hearty chuckle and slapped his thigh.

"Okay. So how are we doin' this?"

"I got the cash at home."

I already knew an expense such as this was going to have to be funneled through momma and that this would be a two-step process at best.

"Well, go get it."

"Bank's closed. I'll get it tomorrow. Your car won't be fixed until then anyway. Listen, there's going to be a big bash here tomorrow night. You bring the girl and I'll bring the cash."

"Then what?"

"I'll slip her a little somethin'-somethin' and take her home with me."

"Then I won't be able to get my car until the next day. She'll find her way back."

"No, I guarantee you she won't."

"Hey, you're not going to . . ."

"You don't get to say what I get to do to her."

"I'm her mother you know, I don't want her hurt."

"A little restraint makes everything work out well for me. Now about your headache . . . these are on the house."

He passed me a small snack-sized baggie with ten pills in it. "You like these, there's plenty more. We can negotiate the price later," he said with a wink and a leer, "You're one hot mama. I'll bet that mouth of your is wicked."

He looked up and said, "She's coming back, Have her here tomorrow night for the party and you can be on your way with a full purse, if you know what I mean." He was offering me both money and drugs for my daughter as if he did this all the time. And women accepted. What a sad commentary for our times, I thought, but had to let it go and get back into character.

"Okay. Just don't think I'll settle for less, 'cause I won't. Have it all."

"I will." He stood to let Vanessa into the booth but Vanessa had other ideas and instead sat and shoved me over in my seat.

I made an oomphing sound to show my displeasure.

"If you didn't have such a fat ass they'd be plenty of room on this seat," she mouthed. "Hey, if you're not going to smoke that, I'll take it."

She took the cigarette where it was sticking up in the mayonnaise, wiped it off on a napkin and put it to her lips. She waited until Junior lit if for her then she blew smoke right into my face. "You're such a loser. You bargain for a cigarette then don't even smoke it. You just wanted to get fucked right?"

I couldn't help it, I don't know what came over me, but I reached up and slapped her, and it was a pretty good one, too. As Vanessa's head snapped back I saw the tiniest glimmer of a smile on her lips. She'd set me up. She knew I'd negotiated the deal and now she wanted to show that our animosity for each other was real. She didn't want him to have any doubt about what was going down.

Junior stood with new admiration in his eyes. I could see his pleasure in discovering he'd have a feisty one on his hands tomorrow. He tossed money down for the meal we'd eaten. Then he handed me two twenties. "There's a motel across the street and down a block. If you two don't kill each other, I'm having a birthday party for my momma here tomorrow night. I'd take great pleasure if you'd both come."

"Cool. A party. Will there be a band? I'd like to hook up with one and be a groupie. You know, have wild sex with all the band members every night."

"You've got yourself a handful here, don't cha?" he said.

"Teenagers . . . what are you going to do? Can't even give 'em away, nobody wants 'em," I replied and smiled as he winked at me. I folded the money he had given me and stuck it in my cleavage. "Thanks for the cash."

"No problem, Sugar. There's more where that came from."

"You got a new friend, huh? Does that mean he's coming back to the room?" Vanessa asked with a snide look.

"No, not tonight. Tomorrow maybe. Let's get out of here, I could use some sleep."

Vanessa followed me out the door and across the street. She popped gum and flipped through all the souvenir brochures on the counter while I registered then she skipped after me going up the outside stairs. Once inside the room, with the door bolted, she grabbed me and hugged me to her chest. "You were terrific!"

"Uh, why thank you," I said as I backed away from this deranged split personality. "Sorry I hit you."

"No problem. I was counting on it actually. God, does Brick know how good you are at this or was this just blind luck?"

I shrugged. "Blind luck I guess. This is all new to me."

"Well you missed your calling, I'd partner with you any day."

I felt myself flush with pride. "Thanks."

"So, what's the scoop? What went on while I was in

the head?"

I filled her in then went to the bathroom myself. When I came back Vanessa said she had talked to Brick and Joe, his team leader and said they agreed that I had played everything just right. It was all on tape and would be used as evidence at the trial. I asked what we did next and she said we had to try to get some sleep without removing our makeup or clothing. There was no one here to put us back together and the wires had to stay taped in place. We would both try to sleep on our backs and then tomorrow we would hang around the motel room until they kicked us out. Later, in the evening, we would show up at the bar, join in on the festivities and after the exchange we would be able to get out of these hideous outfits.

Vanessa and I laid on our double bed on our backs talking way into the night like girls at a slumber party. She was a very sweet girl who had always wanted to join the F.B.I. but at the time she graduated they weren't hiring so she had taken a state position in the same division as Brick and was currently on assignment in Florida where she said child abuse cases were her specialty since there was no shortage of perverts. We talked about my situation. Her being with the agency, she knew all about Jared and his latest attempt to treat me like a caged animal. I spent a lot of time answering her questions and telling her about our courtship. Along with me, she couldn't believe a romance that was so fairy-tale perfect from the outset could turn out so deadly and be such a nightmare.

I knew from Brick that Jared's attorneys had posted the astronomical bond required so he could be out to manage his chain of jewelry stores until his trial and that he had to wear a monitoring device, something my team of attorneys had been adamant about. The press had glommed onto the story and we'd even made a corner snap shot on the cover of *People* magazine, but thankfully, as I was in the hospital at the time, I hadn't had to worry about the press hounding me. For the inside story the press had managed to come up with an old picture of me, one from my college graduation, our wedding photo, and the one Jared had circulated when he was offering the reward for my whereabouts. I really didn't have to worry much about being recognized. I had gone back to my natural blonde hair coloring and now I sported a deep tan from spending so much time outdoors, and I had lost that "fragile" look. Riding bikes, taking long, arduous hikes, and fending for myself doing all the campground duties required when full-time Rving, had made a muscular dynamo out of a bony socialite. I still had all my former grace and agility, but now I had some power behind it. I was probably at the peak of my physical capabilities and it showed in my newfound confidence—which I currently needed to dumb down for this trashy tramp role.

We both fell asleep sometime after three and woke to a sunny day just as the maids were knocking on the doors to oust everyone. I was not thrilled to be wearing the same clothes and unable to shower but chocked it all up to the line of duty. Vanessa and I used what little money we had to go to the diner for lunch and to show anyone who cared to look, that we, as mother and daughter, hated each other's guts.

Chapter Six

The party at Desperado's was in full swing when I ostensibly towed Vanessa behind me. I saw Junior at the bar yakking it up with his cronies and he flashed me a wicked grin and a wink so obvious it scrunched up one side of his face. The man was vile, just plain vile. And I couldn't wait to have this charade over with so that I could see that smug smile wiped off his face. With any luck at all, I might even be lucky enough to get a slap of my own in. That was my supreme thought as I "fought" with Vanessa and nursed a beer.

Junior motioned for me to join him and after slipping my hand down to reassure myself by tapping on the microphone hidden inside my belt, I scooted off the bench and heard Vanessa whisper under her breath, "Here we go."

I sidled up to him and he snaked his arm around my waist. Again that putrid outdoorsy smell and body odor assailed me and I had to force myself not to wince and draw back.

"C'mon babe, take a walk with me," he commanded and before I knew what was up, he led me through the tiny kitchen and out the back door. I remembered in a flash that Brick had told me that no matter what, I was not to leave the building, but I couldn't see any way to accomplish this little transaction if I appeared suspect to his motives and at this point, I really wanted to nail this guy. Plus, I was really hoping he smelled better in the fresh air.

Behind the bar was a dumpster and a small path beside it led to a patch of moonlight glimmering on water. I could see nothing but darkness beyond that. Junior gripped my elbow and led me toward the worn trail. A feeling of dread washed over me. When he gripped me tighter and pulled me along faster, it escalated.

"Hey!" I shouted. But it was too late. We'd reached a clearing and there was a boat anchored at a dilapidated quay.

"Let's go for a boat ride," he said.

"No, I'm afraid of the water and I don't like boats."

"Tough."

I opened my mouth to scream and a wadded handkerchief was stuffed inside. My initial thought was, *Oh, good God, where in the world has that thing been,* before I was shoved into the boat. Barely able to break my fall by catching myself on hands and knees, I fell over and landed ass up.

"Nice," he murmured. "I expect to see you in that position many times."

"In your dreams," I mumbled around the rag as I stumbled to my feet. Big mistake. The tiny bass boat began to shudder and I swayed back and forth. I had to drop to the seat to avoid falling overboard.

I heard a cord being whipped out and an engine catching. I almost fell forward from the impact of the boat being thrust forward and out into the open water. *Shit* was the first word out of my mouth when I managed to dislodge the wad from my mouth and toss it away. If Brick was listening—and he sure as hell better be—I could imagine the curse word he was using was much, much worse.

An evil gleam shone in Junior's eyes as he sat in front of me, his right hand behind him on the tiller. I tried to keep myself calm by remembering how many agents were nearby. Knowing they could all hear what was going on, I was more determined than ever to get what I needed on tape.

"Did you bring the money?" I yelled, acting naïve—as if Plan A was still on the agenda.

His eyebrows rose as if wondering how I could have missed the point in all this. He backed off the power so we could talk but he still kept us moving at a decent clip.

When he just stared and said nothing I asked, "Where are we going?"

He let go of the tiller and we coasted a few feet in silence before he spoke.

"We're going to the Justice of the Peace over in Lexington. Then I thought I'd take you to the Injun casino in Miccosukee for our honeymoon."

"What!"

"You heard me. We's getting' married."

"Oh no *we's* not! You're giving me money for Vanessa."

"Well now here's the sad tale about that. Momma refused to give me the money. Instead she sat me down and told me she thought it was time for me to settle down. It's her birthday today and she wants a grandchild or at least the promise of one. Seems Judge Potts has an envelope of cash for me from Momma that I get as soon as I make you my wife. And Momma's promised me another bit fat one when I get you pregnant. So . . . much as I'd rather have the lovely Vanessa, I gots to make do with you."

This could not be happening. "I don't want to marry you. In fact I refuse to marry you!"

"Believe me, Judge Potts won't give a damn. He owes Momma too many favors to pay any attention to anythin' you have to say. It's a done deed, so you might as well get used to the idea." He spat over the side of the boat. I cringed.

"What you're talking about is called rape."

"I really don't care what you call it. We're doing it. And we will keep doin' it until your belly swells. And if you're any good at it, maybe even after."

I didn't know what else to do, but I was not going to let this pervert kidnap and rape me. I'd already had enough of that to last me a lifetime. I looked over his shoulder trying to gauge how far it was to shore. He saw me and guessed my thoughts. As he sprang up to grab me I knew I would only have this one chance. I leapt up, pushed hard against his chest and using the recoil, forced myself to go over the opposite side into the brackish, dark, and bitterly cold water. Momentum carried me forward and I cleared the side, but just barely—I felt my shoe being tugged off.

In the end it turned out to be a rash move. After righting himself, Junior sat back on the flat seat, crossed his arms and waited while I flailed and sputtered and screamed. All to no avail. The water was freezing. I couldn't believe it was this cold, not in the middle of summer, but I felt my arms and legs becoming sluggish almost immediately. The water felt thick, syrupy, and I was covered with some kind of slime. It was coating my neck and my chin as I struggled to keep my head above water. His hand on the tiller, he shadowed me. I doubt it was five minutes before he was leaning over the side helping me back into the boat.

"Finished swimmin'?" he asked with pronounced sarcasm as he tugged me up and over the side. I curled into a tight ball on the metal floor of the boat shivering as if I had touched a live wire and couldn't let go.

Then he moved to the back, restarted the engine, and instantly the little boat lifted high in the water. It bumped with each wave it crested and jarred my chilled-to-the-bone body. With each repeated slam I was jolted off the floor. I could feel pain shooting through me starting at my butt and driving up all the way into my clenched jaw. The wind whipping around in the bottom of the boat stung my eyes, froze my ears and made the wet strands of my hair batter my face until I had to bury my nose in my chest to avoid the harsh stings.

By the time the engine wound down and shifted into a

low drone that filled the otherwise quiet night, I was anxious to get out of the boat and go anyplace that promised warmth.

With any luck Brick would find me before I was married to this backwoods pervert, but knowing my stupid stunt had probably short circuited the electronics I was wearing in my belt, I knew I'd be lucky if he found me before I gave birth to Junior's junior. I shuddered at the thought. I'd have been better off with Jared was the last thing I remembered thinking before I let the cold take me and lost consciousness.

Chapter Seven

When I came to I was in the middle of a bed piled high with ruffled pillows. I could feel them all around me as I shifted and sank even lower in the enveloping fluff. It was like being in a quicksand of quilts. I patted each one, not quite trusting what I was seeing. Above me, encircling a tacky art deco chandelier, were dozens of diaper-clad cherubs playing harps and shooting off arrows. *Where the hell was I?*

Then I remembered the last place I had been and I panicked. I pushed myself up off the mountain of plush and felt pain dart through my eyeballs. I gasped and managed to take in my surroundings before the pain had me falling back onto the old-fashioned brass bed. At first glance I would have sworn I was in a bordello of old, but as my eyes adjusted and I turned my head from side to side, I realized I was in a very prim, yet very overdone bedroom. Was I in a boudoir at a Zsa Zsa Gabor-inspired B&B? *Dear God, tell me the marriage to that wacko hadn't already taken place!* My hand went to my heart and I was instantly filled with dread as my hand connected to my bare chest. I ran my hand down my body. The cherubs on the ceiling with their tiny sashes had more clothing on than I did. I felt my pulse spike and then with what I considered superhuman effort,

I managed to sit up and stay up. *Big mistake.*

The gilt-framed mirror on the dresser reflected an image of a much tousled and stark naked woman that I did not recognize. Then I remembered I had colored my hair, teased it to the moon, pancaked my face with gobs of makeup and even stained my teeth for this gig. I groaned and then my eyes flashed wide as I saw an older women come out of a door behind my image carrying an armful of towels.

"Oh, you're awake. The judge will be so glad."

"W-who are you?" The woman was Aunt Bea if she was anybody.

"I'm Judge Potts wife, Louellen. What a sight you were when Junior dragged you in here. Clothes all muddy, hair dripping on my newly-polished wooden floors, eyes like a raccoon from all that makeup—a sight, I'll tell you that."

"Where are my clothes?"

"I took them off, then I did my best to bathe you. Had a dickens of a time getting that swamp smell out of your hair though, I can tell you that. You're going to have to borrow one of my dresses for the wedding; your clothes won't be dry for an hour or more. I'll find something we can pull together with a belt as I'm a bit more full-figured." That was an understatement.

"Wedding?" I remembered that's what I had been brought here for but I wanted to hear what she'd been told.

"Can hardly believe it myself—Junior getting married! His momma must be tickled to death. Surprised she's not here for it. She's wanted grandbabies for so long. And you," she looked pointedly at my naked form, "I don't suppose you'll have any problems getting them for her. Now, c'mon, let's see what we can find for you to wear."

She walked over to a series of bi-fold doors that had been painted gold and jerked them open. Every floral pattern you could imagine was represented in the flowing housedresses, all frou-froued with lacy collars and sleeves. I fell back on the bed and groaned. *Where was Brick?*

I was really getting worried now. Had they been following us? Did they even know what had happened to me? I knew no "real" judge would marry me against my will, despite what junior had said, so I wasn't all that concerned about the threat of Junior. And I saw no need to continue the ruse if Junior was no longer interested in buying Vanessa, but it seemed more prudent to stay in character. I had to concentrate on getting out of here.

I saw my belt lying over a chair. *Could it still be working?* I stood and accepted the dress that was being offered. I stepped into the voluminous flower garden at my feet. It buttoned all the way up the front, from hem to collar, and was so big it left me gaping at the top. I was swimming in what I supposed was a size 22 cotton confection. But for now, it was covering the essentials—if I kept my hand clenched in the fold at my neckline.

"Can you hand me my belt so I can cinch it in the middle?"

Louellen turned back to the closet and produced a matching belt. I had no option as clearly it was the better fashion choice. I used it to gather the folds of material.

"There now, that looks nice," she said.

A loud bellow came from somewhere outside the door and I watched Louellen transform from sweet nice old lady to a highly agitated nervous wreck.

"Oh, they're ready! We'd better hurry up!"

Then the door flew open, crashing into the opposite wall.

"Louellen! Ain't you got her cleaned up yet? We don't have all day you know! They got to git to Miccosukee for their honeymoon. That's way down there in Florida."

"This here's my husband, the judge," Louellen said, clearly intimidated by her husband who appeared quite drunk. The half-full tumbler dangling from his fingertips and the unsteady sway made it pretty evident that he'd drank his lunch and had kept right on going.

"Judge, there isn't going to be a wedding, I'm not marrying anyone."

He stared at me then blinked with owl eyes, which appeared to cross and uncross as his brows furrowed into a sharp vee. Clearly no one ever defied him; he didn't seem to know how to react. Then his face turned red and he sputtered.

Junior came into the room behind him and grabbed me by the arm.

"You get your ass downstairs or I'll carry you down. We're getting married whether you want to or not. Judge Potts has already been paid and so have I." He patted a fat pocket in his jean jacket. "I'd like to do this before he passes out and he's clearly on his way."

"I am *not* marrying you. I refuse to say the vows."

Junior looked over at the weaving judge. "Just sign the papers Judge, I don't need the words. Just make it legal on paper for Momma so I can take my bride to that fancy Indian hotel she paid for."

"You cannot marry someone who refuses to get married," I said.

Junior came over, pushed Louellen out of the way then bent and threw me over his shoulder. I immediately began pounding on his back and kicking my legs. He gripped my legs tighter, smacked my rump hard, and then clasped his hand around my neck so hard that after a few seconds I saw stars.

"Git me the papers, Judge. We don't need to do this formal-like, just give me something that says we're married and that I kin fuck her."

Louellen gasped and the judge jerked back, eyes wide. But the wad of bills puffing out of his shirt pocket was enough incentive for him to follow Junior down the stairs and start filling out the forms. I was forced to sit in Junior's lap, a hank of my hair wrapped around his fist as he held my head at a painful angle. He began a whispering a litany of all the things he planned on doing to me once we were alone.

"You got that truck ready like I asked?"

"It's outside, filled up, the keys in it," the judge mumbled as he put his stamp on a certificate. "What'd you say her name was?"

He looked at me. The surprise was evident. He'd never bothered to ask and I hadn't volunteered. "Tell the man."

I spat in his face.

His hand reached out and he slapped me so hard that if he hadn't been holding my hair I felt my neck might have broken. He ripped the sash from my dress and used it to tie my hands together while I was still reeling from the blow. Removing the sash caused the balloon of a dress I was wearing to gape provocatively. My breasts were practically on display.

Brick and his team chose that exact moment to break through the door while two agents crashed through the window. In the process I was dumped off Junior's lap and hit the floor jarring my hip. The bodice, which had already been gaping, fell off one shoulder baring a breast.

There was chaos for a few moments while both Junior and the judge were apprehended and then I felt Brick's hands lift me from the floor, his hands not finding purchase in the flimsy material causing him to bare my other breast in the process. His eyes widened and instantly he dragged me to his chest and clutched me to him shielding me from view. His hot breath fanned my ear as he said in an exasperated voice, "What is it with you? Every time I rescue you I find you topless."

I groaned. My head hurt, my face hurt, my hip hurt, and now my pride hurt. And once again I was humiliated in front of Brick's team.

Brick adjusted the dress, pulling it up and covering me and then he took off his jacket and wrapped it around me. I remembered he had done this exact same thing before when he'd rescued me from the basement in my old house where Jared had imprisoned me.

There was a precise order and a very specific agenda as Junior was taken into custody and read his rights. The judge and his wife were taken into a room by Brick's boss and two other agents. The door was closed behind them. I wondered what was going to happen to the not-so-loyal public servant and his over-the-top loyal wife. Paramedics were called and while we waited I related the whole story, filling in the gaps when we were incommunicado—namely, when I'd gone overboard. And just as I was being checked prior to being loaded into the ambulance to be taken to the hospital, Vanessa came running up and grabbed my hand.

"God we were so worried about you! When we discovered he'd taken you I thought Brick was going to kill somebody. He drove like a madman when he found out where he'd taken you. The feed actually came back to life for a few seconds while we were driving to get here, and he heard Junior say something about preferring you to your daughter anyway before the static filled the van then faded out to nothing again. Brick cursed up a storm and hit the dashboard of the van hard enough to crack it!"

"How'd he find out where Junior was taking me?"

"Just before we lost the signal, Junior told us where you were going and who you were going to see, and his momma was so proud, she spilled the beans to everyone at the party—said it was too late, that you were probably already on your honeymoon makin' her a grandbaby when we questioned her. I never saw Brick so angry. He lifted her up by her throat to move her out of his way and just dropped her."

"We didn't get him though," I moaned.

"Oh yeah we did. He's going down. We got him for assault, kidnapping, corruption, bribing a public official and possession of child pornography. He had a rucksack full of kiddie porn in that boat, *and* it looks like he's the featured star in a lot of the films. He'll be put away for at least twenty-five years, maybe longer."

"Well that's good news."

"You betcha. And we couldn't of done it without you."

"I screwed up."

"No you did not. No one could have anticipated that he

would have preferred you to his normal fare. Although I'm a bit pissed that he liked you better than me."

"No, he didn't. His *momma* liked me better than you, and when it came down to it, he's a momma's boy. She's dangles the purse strings to get her way. And she wanted me to go off with her boy and make her a baby. Thank God you guys found me before he could make his momma a grand momma." I laughed and she hugged me tight.

Brick strode up just then and clasped the hand I held around her shoulder. Vanessa and I broke apart then and he smiled down at me, "Wherever she goes, trouble follows." Then he leaned down and whispered so only I could hear, "Something about you makes men want you." His voice was rough; I could hear the desire in it. "Of course, it would help if you'd stop flashing your tits."

I cringed at the memory and dropped my head in my hand. He laughed. "Let's get you checked out, then I want you in my arms all night so I'll know exactly where you are so I can get some sleep. God I'm tired, how 'bout you?"

"Yeah, and I can't wait to get this stuff off my teeth and out of my hair."

"You look cute all skanked out. But I do miss the blonde, although it turns out you're ditzy no matter what color your hair is. I can't believe you went overboard." He shook his head while he ran his fingers through my hair at the scalp line; it felt good, in both a possessive and physical sense.

I gave him a narrow-eyed glare. How dare he call me ditzy after all I'd done for *him*. He squeezed my hand and laughed.

Two medics lifted me into the ambulance. I had a sense of déjà vu. This was how we had parted last time he'd rescued me. Before I could ask, he shoved someone aside and hopped into the back of the ambulance just as the doors were closing.

It turned out I had to stay overnight as I had taken a pretty hard hit to my face and had some neck trauma. After cleaning up and doing his reports, Brick came back to see me. I was drifting in and out of a fitful sleep. He lifted the covers, slid in beside me and gathered me in his arms. I loved the way he smelled and the way he made me feel safe and comforted. It was the best night's sleep I'd had in weeks.

Chapter Eight

The next morning I was alone when a nurse came in to check my vitals. She didn't know where Brick had gone but had been told by the night duty nurse that he had held me in his arms all night and everyone who'd checked on me thought it was the most romantic thing they had ever seen. Then Brick came in with a loaded cardboard tray from the local Hardee's, and I actually sighed when he bent and kissed me full on the mouth.

"'Mornin' sunshine. Got you a sausage biscuit and some real coffee."

I looked up into the handsome face of a man who had slept well. The staff thought it was because of the woman he held in his arms all night, I thought it was because he was at peace with the little girl in the video I'd seen. He'd finally put her tormentor in jail and this time he was going there to stay.

"You're mighty chipper," I mumbled, conscious of the fact that I hadn't brushed my teeth yet and that my normally pearly whites were a dingy yellow-gray and I still had mile-high Brillo hair. What must these nurses be thinking of Brick's taste in women?

"I am. Guess who's been picked to drag Junior's fat ass back to Kentucky?"

"Hmmm . . . the arresting officer?"

"No, I gave Bobbie, the collar. He's the one who got the hell knocked out of him on account of me last week. Guess again."

"Vanessa."

"Good God no, she's on her way back to Florida. This isn't even her jurisdiction."

"Okay, I give. It's not you is it?"

He beamed at me. "Yeah. I get to be the last face he sees before he's in the system for good."

"Isn't that a little dangerous?"

He gave me a questioning look. "I think I can handle it. He will be in chains you know."

"I meant, isn't it dangerous for him? Won't you be tempted to beat the shit out of him?"

"Oh yeah. But I won't be doing this alone. We normally transport prisoners in teams, but with someone so high profile, who many have a grudge against, we double the team, there'll be four of us."

"Ah. So, when does all this take place?"

"Tomorrow. So you have to get out of here today." His eyebrows went up and down in a get-my-drift kind of way and I laughed out loud.

"I'm told the doctor will be here in about an hour. You can ask him."

"I've got a gun. There will be no asking."

"Well if you have plans of the carnal nature, it ain't happenin' with a skanky woman."

"Thought you'd say that so I brought you a surprise."

"You mean other than the biscuit and mud-in-your-eye coffee?"

"Hey, don't knock the beverage cops are weaned on, couldn't do a stake out without it, ya know. Juanita, get in here!"

From around the edge of the huge door, Juanita popped her head. "S'alright to come in, now?"

"You bet. Juanita, Jenny needs undoin'. Whatever you did the other day, make it go away. I want my beautiful girl back, and while I'll take her anyway I can get her, I would prefer it if she's a blonde again."

Juanita strode into the room with two huge suitcases. "No problem. Gonna take a while though so why don't you just mosey on down to the gift shop while I do my magic."

"Gift shop?"

"This woman's going to need some clothes. If you'll recollect, she came in here with a dress on that could fit a baby elephant. I've been hearing all about the eyeful you got for being the first one to get to her. And mind you, there's a few who are downright unhappy that you didn't share the view."

I blushed and he grinned.

"What size you wear sugar? I'll get you something really nice."

"Six petite if you can find it, or extra small if they're not numbered. And nothing orange, I do not do orange. Remembering the dress I'd come out of, I hollered at his back, "And no flowers, you hear me, no flowers!"

The nurse came in as he went out. "Why don't you want flowers, honey? Hell you deserve them for all you went through."

"I meant no flowered clothes, he's getting me something to wear home."

"Speaking of home, the doctor looked at your chart, you're free to go. When you're ready I just need to call for a wheelchair."

Juanita piped up, "I need her and that bathroom for about an hour, any problems with that?"

"Nah, take your time. We don't have a waitin' list. At least not yet. Now if you'd come during a full moon . . ." her voice drifted off as her clogs quietly cushioned her progress as she crossed the room and closed the door behind her.

An hour later I was back to my old self, with the exception of my outfit. Leave it to a man to buy leather and lace. Something I knew without a doubt he hadn't found in the hospital gift shop.

Chapter Nine

We were flown back to Hillvalley in a helicopter, landing in the middle of Main Street right outside the door to the sheriff's office I had been in just a few days ago. My blue and white Dolphin was still in the parking lot looking out of place next to squad cars and unmarked police cars. Brick got the keys and drove us over to the local K.O.A., where his rig was still set up. I noticed he took a grocery bag off the helicopter and suspected we were dining in.

It was nippy in the mountains but Brick had assured me he was planning on keeping me warm tonight. He had to leave to escort his prisoner tomorrow and I had to get on the road if I was going to meet Randy at The Rally where I hoped to run into Brick's missing sister. But even though it had been on my mind to tell Brick a few times about my hopefully-not-so-crazy idea, I stubbornly talked myself out of it each time. What if Robert Byrnes and his family, including Jillie, didn't show? What if I failed to find her? What if all I did was stir up Brick's emotions and create false hope for him and his family again?

So, I'd decided to go with my original plan and go it alone. I was going to find her and then call for back up, or . . . simply kidnap her back. As I was putting away my things and setting up, I idly wondered what the jail time was for kidnapping a kid who had been kidnapped in the first place. It was certainly a quandary, kidnapping a child is a crime, a very bad crime. I could easily end up in jail over this, or killed should there be a manhunt. My mind raced—an Amber Alert could be issued and an A.P.B. sent out. In his zeal to make a big arrest some cop might shoot first and ask questions later. Should I really do this, should I take this chance on my own?

As I hooked up the water filter to the spigot and fished in my "necessaries" basement, I made a firm decision. I would go to the rally, get set up, make friends and find my way around. And *if* I managed to locate Jillie, and *if* I saw the right opportunity, I'd base my decision on the prevailing circumstances. If I was lucky and I could make a connection I could depend on with someone in law enforcement, I just might involve him or her, if they were of a like mind. If not, I would be on my own. I was scared just thinking about it. But excited too.

I smiled as I thought of Brick, gathering his sister into a bear hug as she ran down the steps of a plane into his waiting arms and my eyes misted. Yeah, I had to do everything I possibly could to make that scenario happen. I had to bring her home to him. So, if everything worked out, he'd have the surprise of his life waiting for him when we hooked up again. If not, nothing would be lost, except my all dashed hopes and expectations of delivering the absolute most perfect present ever to the man I was falling in love with.

My cell phone rang and jolted me back to the present. I was surprised to see that it was Brick calling me from inside his fifth wheel.

"Anytime you're in the mood, come on over. I've got the steaks marinating and the salad just about put together. Could use a corkscrew though, can't seem to find mine."

"Okay, just give me a few minutes. I need to primp."

"If you're planning on slathering on more make-up, forget it. I want you as naked as I can possibly get you . . .

everywhere."

"Well that's what I have to take care of. Does the word Gillette mean anything to you?"

"Oh, yeah. Good idea. I should go 'Gillette,' too."

"It would be greatly appreciated if you did," I said, hoping my smile came through the line.

"Sugar, there are going to be so many things you are going to greatly appreciate about me tonight. You might want to make a list."

"Ditto." I forced myself to sound confident even though I was anything but. I could not even remember the last time I had *wanted* to make love—about three years after my marriage to Jared was my best guess, and that had been quite a few years ago.

"Mmmm . . . sounds very promising. You don't mind if we keep the game on, do you? I've got money on Carolina."

"Only if you don't mind having a hard on you could use for a horseshoe post all next week."

He laughed and made kissing noises into the phone. I heard him sigh deeply, then in a low, husky voice he said, "Get your ass over here as soon as you can—and all those other luscious parts, too." I saw the screen on my cell go blank and smiled. *To Brazilian or not to Brazilian, that was the question.*

Chapter Ten

When I knocked on his door an hour later, I heard him holler for me to come in. I juggled the homemade dessert I'd taken from the freezer, the requested corkscrew, my keys, and a tote bag containing things I might need if I was invited to spend the night.

There was a lot riding on this from my perspective. Sure I was going to have sex with a man I adored, but we were both emotional wrecks. He, for what he'd been going through for the past five years after his sister had been taken from right under his nose in a mall at Christmas time, and for last week's fiasco of an ongoing case he cared deeply about. Me, for what Jared had put me through, not only while we were living together as husband and wife, but also while I'd been on the road running from him. We hadn't resolved our issues, neither one of us, really. But how long could you put your life on hold when it depended on the futures of so many others? It was time. Brick and I had amazing chemistry together. I was mad for his muscular form, his devilish smile, his unwavering blue gaze, and pheromones that had me sniffing like a vacuum whenever he was in the room. Oh yeah, I was ready.

"Hey, I could use a hand here," I said as I managed to

climb into the RV without the use of my hands.

Brick was by the stove setting the timer. In two strides he was at my side taking everything from me and placing it on the counter. I kept the tote bag on my arm and as I passed the sofa I let it slip to the floor between the sofa and the kitchen counter. I didn't want to broadcast that I was a sure thing even though I'd as much said so.

"Ah, you remembered the corkscrew. How long does this stuff have to breathe before it's any good?" He held up a bottle of Chilean red, a cabernet that was a favorite of mine.

"It's good now, breathing just makes it better—a bit more mellow with the edge of an aftertaste smoothed out. I would decant it now and pour two half glasses. I'm so ready for a drink."

"Yeah, me too. But do you mind if I make one of them a beer. I feel like I need something I can chug instead of sip right now."

"Suit yourself. More wine for me." He handed me my glass and went to the fridge for a beer. I sipped as I watched his muscles flex while he moved things around to get to what he was looking for. His broad back in the tight tee looked powerful. The muscles bulging in his arms as he lifted the twelve-pack, situated it on the shelf and tore the cardboard reminded me how strong he was, causing my womb to clench with desire. The flash of warmth was offset by a shudder I felt tingling down my spine. This man would soon have complete physical control of my body. I had trust issues. Could I do this?

I watched his hands mangling the container, his long fingers grasping the bottleneck and pulling it free. My gaze drifted to his profile where his firm lips pursed with the effort before going slack and full. My hand jerked at my side for I longed to caress his shadowed cheek and stroke his lips with my thumb. His hair, in thick freshly brushed waves beckoned for fingers to run through it to muss it up some. I was mesmerized by everything he was; tall, capable, confident, right down to his jean-clad ass displayed so admirably not a foot from where I stood, taunting me. I couldn't resist the temptation. On its own volition my hand reached out and gripped his firm butt cheek.

I watched as his head swung around and his eyes met mine. He stood, holding the beer in his hand and his heated gaze met mine. I knew he was seeing the longing in my eyes, the vulnerability in my parted lips. I hadn't masked anything, hadn't even tried. I knew my eyes were glazed over with lust for him and that my stark hungry expression had to be conveying my blatant desire to be taken by him and taken right now. He quirked a sideways smile and put the beer back in the fridge. He exchanged it for a small bottle of water that I watched him down in mere seconds.

He wiped his mouth with the back of his hand and stared at my lips. "Now that I'm hydrated, let's take care of a few things I've had on my mind lately." He pulled me to him with one hand wrapping around my waist.

My pulse leapt and galloped off until I felt it beating in hundreds of places throughout my body. His lips took mine and that was all it took—one nerve caught fire igniting another and soon I was molten against his chest. I vaguely remember him taking the wine glass from my hand and placing it on the counter before lifting me in his arms. He took two steps forward, heading toward the bedroom, then back pedaled until he was standing by the stove. He propped me on his hip while his left hand punched a series of buttons on the microwave/convection oven, disengaging the timer and turning off the oven. "Dinner can wait. I can't—not any longer." His lips descended to mine, taking them in a full-mouthed kiss, covering and moving over them. My arms wrapped around his neck and I opened for his thrusting tongue.

Chapter Eleven

Brick placed me on his bed with the gentleness of a man carrying a great and fragile treasure. I looked up into his eyes and saw desire and something else—could it be the same flicker of wonder that I had, the realization that we were finally going to be able to take things further—to share this bliss.

As he stared down at me, he undid his belt and pulled it from the loops of his jeans, then he unbuttoned and unzipped them, but he didn't remove them before following me down to the bed. I sensed this was where his control would lie.

He pulled me into his embrace and his hand fisted in my hair, holding me in place while he ravaged my mouth. I could feel him checking his control, fighting with the beast inside to rein it in while his lips feasted and his tongue slid into every crevice it could find. I felt that he didn't just taste me, but that he was imprinting me—somehow marking me as his. With his thumb on my chin he forced my neck to arch while his warm lips traced the hollow at my collarbone, then up the side of my neck to the sensitive spot just under my ear where he lingered and whispered, "I have never wanted a woman like this, never had a burn that just wouldn't go away no matter how far I got from you."

I shivered as much from his words as from what his tongue was doing as it glided around the back of my ear, licked my lobe and then rimmed the opening. When he breathed into my ear and thrust his tongue inside I gasped and arched my hips into his groin. He did want me. The evidence was unmistakable.

I felt his fingers, sure and experienced, unbuttoning my shirt, splaying it wide and deftly unhooking the center clasp on my bra.

"Ah, there are my beauties. I dream about these." His thumb and finger pinched my nipple and I came up off the bed only to be brought back by his hand still fisted in my hair.

"Oh, no, this time you are not getting away." I looked up in time to see his glazed eyes move down my body, assessing his prize. His big hand cupped my breast and lifted it while his head ducked and his lips took charge. "Luscious. You are luscious."

My nipple was already peaked from his tugging on it, but now it was connecting like a live wire to my vagina causing it to clench with want. I moaned. He chuckled with satisfaction.

"Like that do you?"

I managed to sigh my approval.

"Well that's good, because I can do this all night."

A sob burst from me as his teeth nipped the bud that was now as hard as a drill bit, then his lips sucked the nipple and the whole areola into his mouth. While he pulled and tugged with firm lips, the hand holding my head moved down the side of my face, caressing my cheek, my jaw and my neck before covering the other breast and kneading it.

I was in heaven, as turned on as I'd ever been in my life. I wanted him to keep doing everything he was doing, but at the same time I wanted his hand between my legs, touching me in places I only allowed B.O.B. to go these days. I was getting the distinct impression that tonight I wouldn't need four double-A batteries to bring me off, and that if all went well the real McCoy might soon replace my battery-operated boyfriend.

It was curious that my woman's mind was trying to make

a permanent connection to this man before even allowing him entrance to my body. What was it about him that made me want to bind him to me and keep him in my universe forever? Was love doing this? Was it my going-on-thirty ticking clock? The fact that I was at my sexual peak?

He released my nipple and slid his tongue across my breast, between the valley to the other nipple, standing at attention waiting its due. As soon as his mouth clamped around it, the zing that fed my nervous system and flooded my pussy jolted through my brain. *I adore this man. I will worship at his feet. I will allow him any and all liberties he chooses to take. My body is his.*

I felt his hand grip mine, pull it up over my head and then I heard something snap around my wrist. "No," I whispered.

"Yes," I felt his breath at my ear, his lips kissing my face. "I want you vulnerable, open, completely in my care. You trust me don't you?" He lifted onto his elbows and looked into my face, his eyes assessing me, monitoring my response.

I looked deeply into his, seeing the passion and the concern. "Yes, but Jared . . ."

"I am not Jared, and the sooner you learn that the better." Cold metal closed over my other wrist and his hand raised mine to join the other at the top of the bed. His eyes didn't leave mine as he checked the handcuffs. I looked up over my head, one set of cuffs was attached to another and both were hooked over a curlicue in the metal trim at the top of the padded headboard. I could get away by unhooking myself if I really wanted to—he was giving me that at least.

"I will never hurt you. Now I need you to relax and let me enjoy myself. Next time, I may even let you cuff me . . ." his voice was muffled by his lips, dragging down my chest and moving slowly toward my stomach. His hand patted mine and then his fingertips trailed down an outstretched arm, tracing it on the tender inside before toying with my armpit and cupping a breast. His mouth moved lower until my jeans stopped his progress. Instantly he was up, stripping me of both my jeans and my panties. As he tossed them aside he stood and admired my newly shaved mound. "Mmmm . . . dessert first tonight."

He gripped an ankle in each hand; spread my legs wide and knelt between my thighs. I flushed from embarrassment. As his hands slid down to my inner thighs and opened me even more, I squirmed from the humiliation. "No, no, don't."

"Shhh . . ." he cooed. "I just like to see what I'm getting ready to eat."

Thick fingers parted my lips then slid up and down inside my slit, spreading the moisture. And even though I was handcuffed, my legs wide and open to both his gaze and his touch, I was in awe of him and what he was doing to my body. Heat flooded my core and I couldn't remember ever being this wet, this ready.

"Beautiful," he murmured. "You are the loveliest of flowers and now, I'm going to sample your dew." He slid down until he was lying flat between my legs, reached under me, gripped my cheeks and lifted me to his mouth. From the moment his lips touched me, kissed me, suckled me, I was his. Nothing had ever felt this wonderful. I had never felt this cherished. While he explored and feasted on me, I learned what being vulnerable was all about and why he had thought it so important to make me that way—for him. I was being forced to be open and available to him, to letting him have control over my body as if it belonged to him. My arms, though not truly incapacitated, were symbolic of my complete submission. He could do as he willed. I had no choice. But also, I could relax and enjoy everything he was doing, I didn't have to participate, couldn't participate. I was like the Queen of Sheba, being ministered to and taking, only taking from the slave that was between my legs learning with his tongue every nuance of my most private places.

One long finger slid inside me and held. It was joined by another. I arched to press them in deeper, to get them to do more than fill me. But he refused to move them, to fuck me with them. I mewled in protest. I wiggled my hips and ground them into his hand. I could no longer stand the fullness without the pressure. I needed that elusive touch, I absolutely had to have it. So I begged, "Please . . ."

I was writhing in waves of pleasure as he lapped at me, using the flat of his tongue to dab on my clit. I was in full orgasm mode when I felt something press against my anus. The gentle prodding became an insistent thrust and when his finger breached the rim every nerve in my body jumped the track and exploded. One orgasm led to another like firecrackers exploding on a string. The burn ignited one and it burst, sending spasm after spasm careening through me as his fingers and lips milked me.

When I could open my eyes, I felt his hand caressing my mound, his thumb circling around my ultra-sensitive clit. His tender touches on my inner thighs, hips and buttocks, were a welcoming gesture, bringing me back to earth after such a mind-shattering series of orgasms. His eyes met mine as he levered himself up and climbed up my body until his hips were seated against mine. His heavy-lidded gaze flared with desire as in full push-up mode he bent and kissed me. I could taste myself but only marginally as at first he seemed stingy with imparting my essence, and then all bets were off, his tongue thrust in and out of my mouth so forcefully that I knew it was a warning, a precursor to what was coming if I didn't stop him. And no way was I going to stop what was sure to be an amazing union of our bodies. I arched my hips into him and closed my legs so I could squeeze his erection between my thighs, milking him. His hand reached between us and he positioned himself. And then I felt him enter me.

A man who groans as if life has just given him the best reward does wonders for a woman's ego. From the moment he showed his immense pleasure with me, I was only focused on hearing that wonderful sound again. No matter what I had to do to get it. Hampered by my hands being trapped above my head,

I only had my core and legs to work with as he plunged into me over and over again, pushing me deeply into the mattress with each forceful pump.

A quizzical look crossed his face; it was as if he was trying to figure something out. I know he hadn't expected me to be this tight, but this really hadn't been Jared's favorite place. I arched my pelvis up to meet him, letting him know by the insistence of my hips that I was not the least bit uncomfortable with anything he was doing. And then, hands griping the sheets beside my head, he began a fierce, short series of thrusts that brought his nipple within range of my mouth. I glommed onto it, sucking and pulling it away from his chest with my cheeks caved in around it. He jerked, cried out and damned near drove me through the wall. And he groaned.

That wonderful male groan filled the room as he filled me. His nipple, still in my mouth, I looked up at him. His jaw was clenched tight; his eyes closed against the world as he emptied himself and shuddered. I felt tears flood my eyes at the wonder of this man, this man who saved me, this man who filled all of my thoughts and now, filled all of me, body and soul.

His big hand curved around my breast as he slumped off to the side and fell beside me. He reached up and slid my wrists off the metal holder and then flicked open each cuff. He caressed both wrists and brought each one to his mouth for a tender kiss before placing each one on my belly. Satisfaction glimmered in his dazed eyes as he turned me and pulled me into his chest, my nose rubbing against the hair on his muscled pecs. He tightened his arm around my back and with the fingers from his other hand he tipped my chin up to so he could see my face. "You are amazing."

"Ditto. I have never come like that."

He chuckled, "I don't think I've ever been more involved in a woman's orgasms as I was in yours. It was as if I was coming with you, herding you along."

"I didn't know it could be this way."

"Ditto," he whispered as he kissed my cheek. The next thing I knew he was asleep. I watched him, magnificent in every way. Like a conqueror of old, he'd earned his respite. He was in need of recharging. Like a damsel of old, I was wide-awake and eager for validation of our tenuous bond. I wanted more of the afterplay, the flowery language of love telling me how cherished I was. But as a modern day woman, I knew the time for sweet nothings was past for the time being. The best thing I could do to earn his charming soul and to win a replay of something from his amazing sexual repertoire would be to get up and fix his dinner. I got out of bed, covered him with a sheet, closed the door between the bedroom and the bathroom and went to work setting myself to rights. Then I threw on one of his shirts and went out to the living area to get dinner ready. It was a few minutes later, as I was stirring the marinade that I noticed I was humming. I sat with a thunk on the bench of the nook. I realized that this was the first time in a long time that I was truly happy—unbelievably, ecstatically happy.

I went to my RV and found my cell phone and called my mom and then my sister. I don't know why, but I felt I had to share the love that was bursting out of me. After so many years of being sad and having nothing good to report, I was anxious to give the *all's well* to my family, to let them know all was right with my world.

Five minutes later, all the joy was sucked out of my little world.

Chapter Twelve

I realized I had jinxed myself. I'd had mind-blowing sex with an incredibly sexy hunk and now I was going to pay for it. While I'd been doing the deal with Junior, Jared had sent a copy of *The Washington Post* to my parent's house. On the front page was a smiling picture of him and the news that he had been arraigned, but instead of binding him over for trial, they had allowed him to make bail. A staggering amount for most people, but not for Jared, whose chain of jewelry stores had actually benefited from the scandal and his arrest. It was great PR for his new bondage and dominant line.

I thumbed down the contact listing in my cell phone and selected my attorney's number. How had this happened? The man had sodomized, beat me, and held me prisoner in the basement of the home we used to share for over a week! A number of people in law enforcement, including Brick, had assured me he was going to be in jail for a long time and that I no longer had to worry about him tracking me down and finding me again. I'd been assured that I could travel openly and without fear.

Once again, Jared had used his charm and influence and now I had to pull my head and tail in and get back under my shell, like a turtle about to get run over by a bulldozer. I was seething. The article had mentioned the name of the judge who had conditionally released him. Men were so incompetent sometimes—a woman would never have done this!

I'd tried to feign indifference with Mom, because I didn't want to worry her, but when I got my attorney's voicemail, I let him have it. First, for second-guessing the legal system and being woefully wrong, and second, for not being the one to inform me that my stalker husband was free to taunt me and possibly worse. He'd been out for several days already!

By the time I made it back to Brick's RV and checked the potatoes in the microwave, I was so despondent that I didn't even hear him come up behind me. I jumped out of my skin when he put his hands on my upper arms and leaned in to kiss the side of my neck. "Hi, Sugar, what are—" was all he managed to get out before I spun and lashed out with arms flailing. Thank God his reflexes are superhuman and he managed to cage one hand and deflect the blow by the other.

"Whoa! What's all this about?"

He captured both of my hands in his and pinned me against the counter. His voice was feral. "Most women fawn all over me after lovemaking, I've even found a few doodling my name after theirs on napkins. I at least expected you to be friendly, not out for blood."

He must have seen the fear in my eyes for his voice softened, and his fingers drew an errant wisp of hair behind my ear. "What's up, Sugar, what's happened?"

"I thought you were Jared," I sobbed.

He gripped my shoulders and held me away from him so he could stoop and look into my tear-filled eyes. "Jared? I thought we were done with him. What's happened now?"

When I didn't say anything he shook me lightly and said, "Tell me!"

The tears overflowed as I filled him in, choking on the anger and the fear.

Chapter Thirteen

After he heard what I had to say, he dragged me over to the little nook in his kitchen, sat on its edge and pulled me onto his lap. "I'm sure you're not getting the whole story. Let me make a few calls."

I sat on his lap while he punched in numbers, talked to his contacts in Virginia, and ran his fingers lovingly through my hair.

When he snapped his phone shut after the fourth call, he turned me to face him and lifted my chin so he could look me in the eyes. His were serious, but not all that concerned, so I was a bit relieved. I'm sure mine were bloodshot by now.

"It's not as bad as it sounds. He has an ankle monitor and he has to check in once a day with Fairfax County."

"Physically?" I asked.

"Well no, not physically. He has to check in by phone."

"He's a master jeweler, for God's sake! He has every tiny tool know to man, and he's smart. So smart . . . you guys don't even know! That's not going to stop him! It probably won't even slow him down."

"Sure it will. These things are foolproof."

"You don't know him, he'll find a way. He'll be the one

to show you guys who the fools are. Trust me, *he's* no fool. He'll get away."

"Not unless he wants to cut his foot off."

I sniffed and lowered my head as I whimpered. "I wouldn't put it past him."

He chuckled. "Hey, I'm famished. I thought you were getting our dinner started."

"That was the idea, before I got it into my head to call Mom."

"Well, get it back into your head. I need to refuel for part two. Jared is history. He's got some serious legal stuff going on, he's not going to chance getting locked up forever by running you down again."

"I wish I was as sure as you are about this."

"He's toast baby. We got him dead to rights. Ten agents saw him, saw what he'd done to you, and heard him threaten you. When this goes to trial, he hasn't got a prayer."

"You're sure?"

"Hey, I admit, I trust the system more than most. But even though he does have money and influence, there's too much evidence against him to just sweep this under the rug. He's going to get jail time." He stood me up and swatted my backside. "Git ma dinner ready, girl! I'll work on the steaks while you do that magic thing you do with the salad dressing."

I smiled back at him, and nodded. The "magic" I did was to mix some sour cream, mayonnaise and sweet relish with some Chili Sauce.

"So, on to round two after dinner, eh? The real McCoy's going to be up to it?" I asked.

"Who?"

"McCoy. It's the name I've given your . . . well you know . . ."

"My penis?" he choked on the beer he had just put to his mouth.

"Mmm, yeah."

"Care to elaborate?"

"As in the real McCoy."

"As opposed to?"

"The fake McCoy. Bob."

"Bob? Who's Bob?" I could hear anger in his voice.

"B-O-B. Battery Operated Boyfriend. My nightstand handyman."

"Oh. The standby. Or in this case, the stand-in."

I laughed. "Well actually the stand-*on*. He just needs to be touching certain places."

"Mmmm. Let me guess which places . . . baby toe?"

"No, not even warm."

"Elbow?"

"Umm. Nope."

"Nose?"

"Unnhuh."

"Belly button?"

"Closer."

"Ahh. Your vagina, maybe?"

"No, but you're very, very close. When you use a Bob where do you put it?"

"I don't have a boyfriend, Bob or otherwise."

"But if you did?"

"I guess if I had a toy that would do anything I wanted, I'd want it to suck the head of my penis. I don't think they make anything like that."

"Well actually they kind of do. It's sort of a suctiony thing, you fit it over and sort of tug and it feels like . . . well sucking, I suppose. I've never seen it in person, just online."

"Really? Where can I get one of those? And where have I been that I missed this amazing invention?"

I pouted my lips and feigned indignation. "I thought I did an admirable job a few days ago."

He grabbed me around the waist and pulled me close. I could smell his aftershave and the essence of him that was allman on his neck. I breathed deeply trying to absorb it, to settle it into my core. "You're not always handy, but I definitely prefer you to anything manufactured. How about you?"

"How about me what?"

"Do you prefer me to Bob?"

I leaned up and kissed him on the chin. "Oh I do, I most definitely do."

He growled and nuzzled my neck. "Food woman! I must have sustenance and then we'll go for round two, three, and possibly even four. I will show you what the real Robert Burns meant when he said, 'by passion driven . . .'"

His lips found mine and he kissed me hungrily. After a few moments, his thumb pressed on the corner of my mouth and he slid it in and used it to rim the soft inside flesh of my lower lip while his tongue explored my upper lip. He held my mouth open while his tongue darted boldly and thrillingly over every part of my lips, tongue and teeth. This was a wild and adventurous side I'd yet to see.

When we broke apart he stared into my face and I gazed back into his. The wonder I saw there was reflected in my eyes. We had just acknowledged that we wanted to be wicked together and the knowledge that we would soon be back in his bed satisfying our curiosity about each other, flared between us. But there was something else, something intrinsic and especially wonderful. Neither of us was ready to talk about that yet—randy, no holds barred sex was one thing, feelings were another.

He patted my ass and grabbed the plate of steaks off the counter. "And I noticed you already took care of dessert."

"Yes . . . I put it in the freezer for later."

"That's not what I was talking about."

When I looked at him with a puzzled expression he cupped my mound. "You didn't think your Brazilian would entice me to nibble? I have a full jar of fudge sauce that's going to be put to very good use tonight."

My eyes went wide and I gasped as his meaning sunk

home, but by then Brick had turned and headed out the door.

We were both quiet over dinner, lost in thoughts of the day and enjoying a meal we were both famished for. Seriously, we were like two pigs at a trough.

I finished first, my eyes clearly bigger than my stomach as I was only able to eat half my dinner. Brick finally pushed his empty plate away and patted his tummy saying, "I'd better stop now so I have room for dessert. I love chocolate. On anything . . ."

His eyes met mine, silently communicating his intent by waggling his eyebrows.

I blushed at the thought and wondered if I should tell him that oral sex from my perspective hadn't been a big favorite for me before. But he seemed so happy with the prospect that I let it go for now. He'd find out soon enough. Unless what had happened earlier hadn't been a fluke. Jared had done me no favors in that department—with his threats and then attempts to install body jewelry, I had not been able to truly relax and get into the pleasure of a man's lips and tongue exploring me down there. Maybe now it would be different.

I washed the dishes while Brick cleaned the grill and then I had to listen to him lecture me on how I was doing it all wrong. I'm sure in his mind he was just enlightening me on the "finer" skills of camping. But really, men have a totally different concept when it comes to conserving water. Passably clean is okay with them, while women like lots of suds and therefore dishes require more rinsing. He was really serious about this as he'd been RVing for quite some time and had been in situations where anything other than bottled water was pretty much non-existent. So I listened, nodded and said I'd do better next time. Mentally, I put a post-it in my head, "Next dinner with Brick, use paper plates."

I was so tempted to ask how the search for Robert Brynes was going; he was the man we believed had his sister. But I knew if I did, I'd end up spilling the beans and telling him all about my plans to find her and snatch her back if necessary at The Rally, where I was heading to next. But I had no chance to even broach the subject as I found myself hoisted by my elbows and carried as if I was weightless, backwards, toward the bedroom.

He leaned me against the wall and touched me with such gentleness, such genuine affection that I shuddered from the sheer pleasure of it. With the barest tips of his fingers he traced every part of my face, ending with my lips that he butterfly kissed until I thought I would melt and slide down the wall. Every nerve in my body was responding to his touch and craving more.

I'd only been with one man until tonight, in the truly intimate way, and that man had been my ex, whose lovemaking had never been particularly tender or loving, but more along the lines of self-serving. And for the last years of our marriage he was rough and demeaning if not downright brutal. Jared's latest attempts at trying to keep me his, and his alone, had been the farthest thing from lovemaking one could imagine. So to have this wonderful unsettling feeling rocking me to my core was heady indeed. I wasn't sure I'd ever have this feeling again. I'd never had it to this extent. Brick overwhelmed my senses, then reeled me back and started all over again. It was like having a fever go in and go out, a tide that enticed and then abated. It made you want more.

His sure fingers flicked open the buttons on my shirt, and tremors, one right after another erupted and jolted through me as his fingertips ran over the tops of my breasts. I felt myself arch and actually willed my breasts to spill out of the cups of my bra and push into his hands. They were not obedient. I looked up into his face and our eyes met. I saw the humor in his as I acknowledged the power he had over my body.

Brick's skill and the cocky confidence he displayed by knowing my body so well excited me to no end. I was overwhelmed by him and the passion he had for me. In those quiet moments when the only thing I could hear was our mingled breath, he gave me something I'd never had . . . affection and a sense of worth as a woman.

I could feel his need and it wasn't just for sex, it was for sex with *me*. My deepest fantasies came true with each feather-light touch, each brushing caress, each moan of pleasure that escaped his lips and mine as he found something new to revel in as he explored my body.

When he had removed every stitch I was wearing, his fingers found me wet and ready and he groaned his pleasure with the discovery. It was enough to burst my galloping heart. Then he lifted me, placed me in the center of the bed and gave me the gift I so desperately needed—pleasure . . . my own selfish, one-way pleasure, given freely it depended on nothing, promised nothing—it was just mine to take. And I relished each kiss, each foray, each swipe and dab of his tongue as my body coiled, sprung and then released. If this was lovemaking, I wanted more of it. As my body throbbed and I listened to my heartbeat begin to settle, I realized all the ways I craved this man—his scent, his touch, the heat of his skin, the very way he breathed. As he climbed over me and entered me with something considerably more substantial than his fingers I realized I was becoming addicted to his lovemaking. I now knew why people did anything, sold anything, paid anything to have this feeling come over them again, and again, and again. I was lost, and at this moment, I was damned sure I did not want to be found.

I was too much in my own little world to get involved with his need to thrust and retreat. But he was determined I wasn't going to be left out and those very talented fingers moved between our bodies as he ground into me making sure all my special places were aroused. Then with a strangled groan, I felt his passion shift. His large hands caged the sides of my face and his mouth took mine. Like a man with a raging fever his tongue delved and thrust trying to capture something elusive, yet I knew not what. At the same time his hips thrust hard against mine, burying his cock deep inside my body. A few frantic pumps and some very crude curse words were the prelude to his body convulsing like a jackhammer against my womb. His fingers, still between us, playing like a maestro on my clit, tugged and with warp speed I joined him in bliss. We were separate yet one, enjoying our passion interlocked in each other's.

It was many minutes, perhaps as many as five before either of us shifted or spoke.

"Kill me now," he murmured against my neck. "I've got nothing more to live for. This is the pinnacle."

"Oh yeah, right. I finally get a man who knows how to ring my bell and I'm going to do him in? Not likely. Although there is a possibility that I might die if you don't get off of me." I pushed against his chest and drew a much-needed breath. He raised himself to his elbows then flopped over on the bed beside me.

I wanted to thank him, praise him, beg for fealty. But instead I felt moisture fill my eyes and run down my face. Horrified, I looked over at him. What would he think? I truly wasn't unhappy. I had no idea why I was crying and I didn't want him to think I was at all displeased about *anything*. I needn't have worried. One look at his totally relaxed face and the regular lift of his massive chest told me he was asleep. And if ever there was a man who deserved it, it was he. I quietly got out of bed, gathered my clothes and went back to my RV to take a shower. I didn't want to take a chance on waking him, and I didn't need another lecture on water conservation. Afterward, aware of his finely honed reflexes, I decided not to chance going back to join him in his bed. We both needed the sleep. Besides, the little experience I'd had with men so satiated, was that they tended to snore most astoundingly.

Chapter Fourteen

I was sitting at my picnic table eating Shredded Mini-Wheats when Brick stumbled out the door of his RV looking anything but well rested.

"Oh, there y'are. Thought you'd run out on me again."

I couldn't blame him; I had done that in the past. "Nope, here I am, just having some cereal and waitin' for you, you sleepyhead."

He walked over dragging his hand through tousled curls. The stubble of his beard was very prominent, stark black against his light tan. Very virile, very sexy, I thought. Then I remembered all the places those erstwhile smooth-shaven cheeks, chin, and jaw had been last night. I felt a blush creep up my face as he rubbed both hands against the stubble trying to wake up.

"Time's it?"

"Ten."

"Shit. You should've woke me. I have to git goin'. Gotta be back on the road by eleven."

"I thought you'd needed the sleep more than anything else."

He sat beside me and patted my thigh. "Well lass, that's where you're wrong. I needed to wake and find you in my bed.

McCoy felt the very same way, I can tell ya."

I laughed. "Would have thought you'd worn him out last night."

He chuckled and reached an arm around my waist and pulled me closer. "Not a chance, he's from hardy stock, McCoy being Scottish you know. We forgot the chocolate . . . thought about maybe having some for breakfast."

He reached over with his other hand and snagged a Mini-Wheat and popped it into his mouth. I watched him chew it, listening to the crunch as his teeth pulverized it, then I continued to watch as he lifted my bowl, put it to his lips and drank some of the milk. His tanned throat worked as he swallowed and for the life of me, I did not know why, that gave me a heady feeling. Did everything about this man turn me on now?

"Hey, I was thinking . . . you want to try something more permanent between us?" He'd said it so causally, as if it had no weight, that my answer mattered not at all to him.

I was flabbergasted. What did he mean by that? Coming out of nowhere, I was totally unprepared. "Uh . . . what exactly do you mean?"

"Shacking up was something that came to mind, but I don't really know how we'd do that with all the traveling I do, and this here being a state-owned vehicle," he waved his hand to indicate his rig.

He was undercover most of the time and used his fifth-wheel and toy hauler pick-up truck to catch the bad guys who were terrorizing little kids in cities all over the country, not just in RV parks, which had more than their fair share of the unsavory type, but in trailer parks and rural communities. The big cities had whole departments devoted full-time to pedophiles and molesters, but the little burgs and travel parks often needed more specialized help. The state provided men like Brick and women like Vanessa who were experts at tracking society's most despicable villains. I knew that it was professionally and personally devastating to Brick that his sister was one of their victims and that he had yet to bring her abductors to justice.

As we both had jobs to do, and I dared not tip my hand about my next mission, I decided to stem this, or more accurately, to stall for now. "Well the logistics of us 'shacking up' might be easier a bit down the road. Right now you have a prisoner to deliver. I have a divorce I have to see to and hopefully a wedding reception for Connor and Diana when he gets back from overseas in six months. Why don't we hook up after The Rally and see what can be worked out? I honestly would not mind having you as a roomie," I said with a knowing smile. "Someone to share the expenses . . ."

"Someone to share my bed . . ."

"I think we've already established that technically you don't own a bed."

"Oh, yeah, right. Someone to share your bed . . ."

"That's better."

"So where are you going? You going to stay here for a few days?" He knew I wanted to get the full RV experience, that I wanted to go to some Samborees, RV expos, and rallies. We'd talked about the seminars and how helpful they'd be to a fledgling like me. I was looking forward to taking cooking classes, caravan classes, even the best-ways-to-clean-your-RV classes.

"No, I'll be leaving later today. I'm going to The Rally in Redmond. I was heading that way when you called. I had just gotten back to Austin to get my RV out of storage and I was heading west when I had to backtrack to meet you."

He scrubbed the back of my neck. "I'm sorry. But I really needed you. I knew you could help me get Junior and redeem me after my major screw-up. When I came up with the plan, Vanessa was the only female agent available. I thought of you right away. But had I known he was going to latch onto you instead . . ." he sighed and shook his head.

"Don't go there. I was glad I could help. I got a taste of the satisfaction you feel when one of these sleezeballs is off the streets. But let that be a lesson to you."

"What?"

"Next time you need me to role play it better not be as somebody's mother!"

"Oh, I have some role playing in mind, and it's not of the motherly type at all."

"Oh yeah? French maid, naughty nurse, teacher's pet?"

"Mmmm. There's merit in all of them, but I was thinking . . . since you'll already be out west, how about meeting me in Sturgis for the Bike rally this year? A Biker Babe in leathers for me to display on my sleeve might be just the reward we both need for a job well done."

"That sounds doable." I knew he kept his Harley in the garage of his fifth wheel and that riding it was his passion. One that I hoped was being usurped by me.

"Great, I'll arrange it. We'll park the Dolphin and take my rig since that's where the bike lives."

"Okay. That's a plan." I was hopeful he'd be reunited with his sister by then and that all this would be moot, as he'd want to spend time with her, not me.

He patted my leg and got up, "I'd better get showered and dressed." He was almost to his door when he turned and looked at me. "By the way, just why are you going to The Rally?"

I praised the heavens that I had planned for just this contingency otherwise I would have stammered and hedged and he would have known I was lying. At least I had rehearsed, I had a chance he wouldn't trap me in a lie.

"It's billed as the Greatest RV Event in the World. They have 150 seminars, I figure, being so new to all this, I may learn more about the camping lifestyle. There's one on how to use your microwave, Crock pot cooking on the road, Cleaning the Micro fiber way, Walking yourself to a better you . . ." He'd already turned and made his way into his RV. *Whew! That was close. The man had a sixth sense for prevarication. It would be good to remember that.*

Chapter Fifteen

I waited until he had washed, dressed, torn down, packed up, and headed out before attending to my own RV. I didn't have to rush, I had over a week to get to Oregon but I was antsy to get on the road and on my way. An opportunity like this might never come again.

In fact, it would be devastating if this opportunity were missed. So much so, that I wondered whether keeping all this to myself was prudent. What would happen if I broke down, had an accident, or somehow became disabled and couldn't get there? Or couldn't tell anyone else?

While I unhooked and stowed everything I mulled this over. I needed a backup plan. Anything could go wrong and the chance to reunite Brick with his sister could be lost forever. And just how would *that* affect our relationship? I'd never be able to face him knowing I'd blown it, even if he never knew it. It would be the elephant in the room that only I ever saw.

I thought about Daniel. He would help if I asked. After all, I had been responsible for him marrying his one true love and living happily ever after. Why, he and Julia even had another baby in the making, one that would be here next spring. But he had a family, and this could be dangerous. He'd been on the wrong side of the law before, and this could put him there again. I thought about Connor. But he was serving overseas, and Diana, his new wife, was in college waiting for his return. Who else did I know who would listen to my hare-brained plan and get involved, or at least be apprised and act as a back up? I had so few friends now, having run away from everything to get away from Jared. And that was another thing; I had to worry about him again. No matter what Brick said, Jared was not going to let a little thing like an ankle "bracelet" stand in his way. He wanted revenge, I had humiliated him, he wasn't going to forget that and play nice.

I thought about my family. Hell, my sister was already on the west coast in Washington State, maybe she would help. We hadn't been all that close since I married Jared, as he had isolated me from friends and family early on, before I'd even become aware he'd been doing it. But I knew she loved me and believed in me. She could be my back up, I decided. She would be the one I confided in and told all to. Then if for some reason I couldn't pull this off, it would be her job to get in touch with Brick so he could take over using the information I had discovered. Yeah, that would work. I felt much better, until I stopped for gas and had to shell out close to three hundred dollars to fill the gas and propane tank. Geez . . . how did families afford this?

An hour later I was on Interstate 75 driving away from the K.O.A. in Corbin, Kentucky and making my way to Lexington where I would pick up Interstate 64 skirting Indiana and Illinois before heading toward Missouri where I hoped to be able to find a nice quiet campground.

It felt great to be back in the driver's seat, sitting high and looking through the windshield at the panoramic view of the mountains all around me. I drove listening to country music for a while as it seemed to be the most popular stuff on the radio in these parts, then switched to a book on CD to while away the hours. It was a good road for the RV and very scenic for me. Apple orchards breezed by and a few signs for country stores sorely tempted me. But if there was one thing I'd learned about RVing, it was you didn't have room for collecting chotskies. I got hungry and stopped at a rest area on Interstate 70, used the bathroom at the travel center and then made a tuna sandwich for a late lunch, which I ate at my nook as I watched all the travelers pulling in to do the same thing. I like this life on the road. Every day is a different challenge and a whole new outlook on life.

I watched a husband and wife in their seventies pull up in their Dutch Star and exit their RV. She came down the steps first, set up a wheelchair, then turned back to help him hop down the steps before gently assisting him into the wheelchair. He had only one leg. I wondered why she would do such a thing; surely they had a bathroom on board. Wouldn't that be easier for her? Then I saw her take something from her pocket, put her fingers to her mouth and blow on a whistle. A big German shepherd came bounding down the steps and brushed up against her leg. The diminutive woman stopped and took the handle for what looked like a working harness. The man pressed a button on his wheelchair and off they went. I soon realized that she was blind. Mostly from the way the man looked up and talked to her and gently touched her elbow, but also by the way she responded each time the dog redirected her. The dog led her to an area beside the sidewalk where he could be walked and did his business. The man backed up and pulled alongside, then used a baggie to scoop it up. He then left on his own to dispose of it. So who was driving the RV, I wondered. Then it dawned on me, he could drive it, as he was only missing one leg, his left one, whereas she was blind and obviously could not. I was flabbergasted. Surely, they could live more comfortably at home without the rigors being on the road required.

I just had to talk to this couple. This was the most amazing thing. What devotion. I left my RV and sauntered over to where the man and woman were. I noticed she had a fistful of buttercups in her hand that she hadn't had before. When I got within twenty feet the dog took notice. When I got within ten he growled and I saw the hair on his neck rise.

"Uh, excuse me," I called. "My name is Jenny, and I'm parked in the RV beside yours, the uh . . . Dolphin." I was always insecure talking about my RV when I was around someone who had one that was four times the price. It was like someone driving a Ford Fiesta approaching someone who just stepped out of a Porsche. You sure couldn't brag about your car much.

Both the man and the woman turned; the dog was clearly waiting for a signal from either before deciding I was friend or foe.

"Yes?" The man said.

"I um . . . was just wondering. You have such a nice rig, so you must be devoted to the lifestyle, and as I'm fairly new to it I often think it's more trouble than it's worth sometimes. Apparently you two, don't. I mean . . . you having to adapt to things more than most."

The woman smiled and the man nodded. The dog visibly relaxed. "You can come closer, Jenny. This is Gallant, he'll be good. He takes his cues from us."

"Gallant?" I asked. Strange name for a dog, I thought, but maybe not for a seeing-eye dog.

"Well, that's what we call him. My husband's name is Rufus."

It clicked immediately. "Rufus and Gallant. *Highlights* magazine!"

They both smiled that I'd made the connection. It was apparently their own little joke. "Yes, he's the good one," she said as she patted the dog and then used her forefinger with the others tucked under it as if pretending to admonish Rufus. "He's the naughty one. Always has been." It was said fondly but there was a hint of melancholy in her voice.

"How long have you been RVing?" I asked. I walked closer but kept Gallant a safe distance away and within my peripheral vision.

"Almost all our married lives," Rufus said. "Helen and I

got our first camper in the fifties, a little Tear Drop. Then when the children came along we bought a Holiday Rambler. Traveled with the kids every summer. So over fifty years."

"Wow. The stories you must have."

"Great memories," Helen said nodding.

"But the kids have their own kids now, 'cept John, who we lost in Vietnam," Rufus said.

"Oh, I'm sorry."

"We all are," Rufus said, dismissing the topic and going on. "This is our last trip, so we're making it last."

"Last trip?" I asked.

"Yes. The kids are making us sell the motorhome when we get back. They think we're too old to be traveling by ourselves."

"Well don't you think that should be your decision," I asked.

They both laughed. "It is dear, we tricked them. We agreed this would be out last trip, but we didn't tell them when we would be back," Helen said with a huge grin.

"How long have you been away?"

"Two years next month."

I hooted and we all laughed. Gallant felt so comfortable with me now that he actually sat at Helen's feet.

"Well I admire you. It can't be easy at times."

"No, but we're together doing what we want to do and not living in a home as our family would like. It's really the only way we can be sure we'll be together. Once you go into those homes, sooner or later they separate you." Helen fumbled for Rufus' hand and he gripped hers when she found it.

"What a great couple you are."

"Well we can tell you, RVing has kept us sane all these years. Whether you need to get away to absorb a tragedy, or celebrate life it's freeing. Getting back to nature, meeting new people, and just having the excitement of being on the road going from one amazing place to another is energizing. We just love it. And until one of us in unable, we plan on doing it to the end." Rufus looked up into Helen's face and I could see the love he had for her. "I lost my leg five years ago when I got a real bad staff infection after a knee replacement. She lost nearly all her sight to macular degeneration at about the same time. If we hadn't had this," his arm swung wide and encompassed the Dutch Star and their matching tow vehicle, a late model bronze Saturn sedan, "to look forward to we'd probably both be gone by now."

"Well thank you for talking to me. You've made my day."

"Well, thankee. You take care, Jenny."

"Is there anything I can do for you, before I head off?"

The woman reached into her pocket and produced a card. I had to come closer to take it from her when she offered it to me. "Yes, you can email my daughter and son-in-law and tell them that we're having the time of our lives, and we'd love for them to bring the grandbabies and come visit us on the road somewhere. Coming from someone else, they may believe it and stop hassling us."

I took the card and looked at it. Rufus and Helen Wilson of Rochester, New York. It had their email address as well as their daughter's. On the back there was a long list of phone numbers under, In Case of Emergency please call:

"They make us both carry them everywhere we go. You could let them know, that as far as parents go we're much more obedient than they ever were as children," Rufus gave a bark of a laugh. "Happy trails!" He punched a button on his armrest and off they went, Helen holding onto both Gallant and Rufus.

Long after they were inside the travel center I stood staring down at the card. Is this what Brick meant by us having something more permanent between us? It was both sad and beautiful. I smiled, tucked the card in my pocket and skipped back to my RV. Life *was* good!

Chapter Sixteen

I found a Flying J and a Denny's at Exit 188 and filled up both the Dolphin and me. I couldn't help but think of Angelina and the time we'd had at the Denny's in Georgia. I remembered she'd ordered the Superbird, which she ate with gusto. I decided to do the same.

Forty miles shy of Columbia, what I figured to be the halfway point across Missouri, I began to feel fatigued and decided to start looking for a place to rest my weary head. The heavy carbs of my Superbird—with fries of course—were taking their toll. At Exit 170 I had to decide between Kan-Do RV Park and Lazy Day RV Park. *The Next Exit* guidebook I'd thumbed through and then purchased while standing in line at the Flying J indicated that both had easy access and were close to the highway. I chose Kan-Do just because I liked the name. I thought it a good sign for my mission at The Rally. They were reasonable at $30 and had full hookups. I noticed there seemed to be a frog theme, and while cute, I was dearly hoping I would not be kept awake by the sound of a multitude of them croaking all night.

I shouldn't have bothered worrying about the frogs. Within minutes of showering after hooking up, I was fast asleep and I doubt a bullfrog sitting by my ear would have disturbed me unless he decided to lick it.

I was up and out bright and early after having plotted my route on MapQuest and then emailing Rufus and Helen's children regarding their status and their request for a visit.

I was hoping to make it all the way to Colorado today, but stories I heard about the foreverness of the Kansas landscape had me doubting I'd make it. I didn't. Not by a long shot. I ended up at Deer Creek Valley near Topeka relatively early in the day because I had a bitch of a headache and just couldn't drive any further. It was a lovely RV park, fairly new and quite the destination place. I had committed myself in terms of the orientation of my RV before realizing this wasn't a cheap place, but for convenience, and because I definitely did not want to turn this sucker around, *and* because the idea of getting back onto the highway made my splitting headache even more, I signed the charge ticket and followed the golf cart around to my site.

I didn't even set up. I didn't even get out of my rig. I left the slide in, ran the A/C off the generator, took four Advil and dove into my bed.

I woke to choruses of, "You're missin' the party, Dixie!"; "Grandma, git the curlers outta yore hair. If this isn't occasion to have it curled for I don't know what is!"; "Momma, stop ironin' that dress, I said I ain't wearin' it!"; "Bubba stop that barkin', it's just a damned frog."

I sat up and rubbed my head. The surroundings were familiar, this was my bedroom, but I didn't recognize one single voice, not even the dog's. Added to all the yelling was the loud noise of a game show and unless I missed my guess it was *Wheel of Fortune*. Had I slept all afternoon?

I crawled off the bed and lifted the blind on the most promising side. Sure enough, Mom, Dad, Grandma, two teenaged girls and a huge bulldog were out in their makeshift living room, complete with a campfire off to the side, and a blaring flat screen TV on a pull-out slide. The man of the house had a bottle of beer in one hand and a remote in the other. *Was I back in Kentucky?*

"The party already started, can't you guys hear the band?" One of the teens wailed. And sure enough, tilting my head I could hear the strains of *Neon Moon* being crooned.

I dropped the blind and made my way up front. The sun was going down but there was still an hour or so of daylight before it was dark. It would be a good time to set the jacks, get the slide out and do all the hook-ups. Then a nice long shower would be just what the doctor ordered.

As I made my way around the RV, checking out this, fixing that, plugging in and setting up I couldn't help but hear the conversation not five feet away. No one acknowledged me except the grandma who smiled without her teeth and then the dog who slowly got up and came over for a sniff. He was old and it was a major effort, so I had to reward him with a few friendly pats.

"The Johnson twins are playin', remember they was here last year. I think Jesse was sweet on Darlene," Grandma said with a grin.

"Hush your mouth Momma, she's only seventeen, he and his brother gotta be gittin' close to thirty!"

"Like ma men with some 'sperience," the older woman grumbled back.

"Your memory's failin' old girl—you's seventy-seven now, but last time I recall, you liked them breathin', that was about all." This from the man sitting in a canvas chair so stretched out from his burgeoning weight that it looked like it was going to let loose any minute now.

If I weren't so afraid my headache would come back, I would have been doubling over with laughter. As it was, I was having trouble just trying to hide my smirk. I finished all my chores, nodded to the teenager who was now glaring at me and went back inside.

The shower revived me and I felt like a new woman. So

new, and so frisky that I thought I'd wander over to the pool pavilion and check out these Johnson twins. I was intrigued. Plus I loved the voice of the man signing Roy Clark's *Come Live with Me*. As far as I was concerned that man wouldn't have to even have a ring if he promised to sing to me like that everyday.

I dressed in jeans and a soft blue button-down shirt with the cuffs rolled back. If there's anything I've learned about camping, it's that nighttime is not a time to show the mosquitoes too much skin. Instead of my usual ponytail I took the time to French braid my hair and insert some turquoise pendant earrings I'd bought in New Mexico.

The music was coming from an area not two hundred yards away, set up in front of the meeting rooms in a building used as a storm shelter and people were literally dancing in the streets. All the sites and roads were paved and people came from all directions in golf carts, wheelchairs, skateboards, and Razor scooters. I watched the teenagers from next door straddling their bikes and mooning over the band members. It was a small group, but they were really good.

A table was set up with BBQ fixin's and I was encouraged by the woman who had checked me in to help myself. I took a plate and put a piece of chicken on it that I picked at along with a corn muffin. I sauntered around and looked at the RVs parked around the perimeter and then I ambled back to the crowds in front of the band.

The Johnson twins were indeed yummy, and as Grandma had said, reeked of "'sperience." Or at least that was what I took their well-placed winks to mean. And of course, they were too old for the girls next door. But I, with my newfound sexuality, was intrigued. Nothing like a man in tight jeans with the obvious package on the front side and a tight butt on the backside—times two and I was in hormone-girl heaven. When break time came and a DJ replaced the live band, one of the twins tapped me on the elbow and invited me to dance. It was a fast two-step and I begged off saying I didn't know how to do the dance that everyone in the big circle was doing. *No* apparently wasn't an option as I was dragged over to the circle, gripped around the waist and introduced to country line dancing. Over the course of two hours I learned to Boot Scoot, Tush Push, Watermelon Crawl, Cowboy, Slap Leather, and of course, Two-step.

I finally had to remind the twins that while they were two, I was only one and could not be expected to be passed back and forth between them and dance every dance. I did manage to corral them into dancing with "the girls next door," and had to smile at the teenager's over-the-moon bright faces. It was a night to remember, for them and for me. I'm sure some cowboy fantasies were etched into young hearts that night. For me, it was flattering to have the attention of two handsome ranchers who could make me damn near melt onto the pavement when they crooned their husky songs into my ears.

At the end of the night, I let them walk me to my door where they flipped a coin among themselves to see who got the goodnight kiss. James good-naturedly backed away while Jesse moved in and pulled me to him. I thought it was just going to be a peck but Jesse thought otherwise and enveloped me in his arms.

"I-I'm not available," I managed to get out before his lips crushed mine.

"He's not either," I heard James say from behind us as Jesse managed to breach my mouth and make a wild foray. "But he is in an open marriage—same with me and my wife, they're both very understanding and happy to share if you get my drift."

My hands were on Jesse's shoulders and I pushed him away. I'm sure my face registered my shock. "Actually I don't. Are you saying you're both married and free to fool around?"

"Not only that, but Janie and Tammie love to participate and join in the fun. You ever done a foursome, honey?"

"Foursome? I haven't even done a threesome. I'm just barely getting back into doing twosomes," I added. These boys *were* 'sperienced. I wondered if Grandma knew just how 'sperienced they were. It was a good thing the teenagers next door were home with mommy and daddy.

"Shame," Jesse said as his fingertips caressed the side of my face.

James sandwiched me from behind and whispered in my ear, "Two is ever so much better than one . . . you should try it sometime."

"No time like the present . . ." Jesse murmured as his lips began a slow circuit down the opposite side of my neck. In tandem they both moved in and I felt the exact same caress on both sides of my neck while one pair of hands fondled my buttocks another skimmed my sides, thumbs caressing the undersides of my breasts and grazing my nipples.

"Uh, fellas . . . I uh . . . mmm, that feels good . . . but I can't." I managed to push off and both men stepped away.

"I got a guy . . . we have an understanding. This wouldn't go over well with him." *Go over well? Who was I kidding? These guys would be mincemeat.*

Both men simply nodded, one kissed my cheek and the other patted my butt and then they slowly sauntered away. But not without a backwards look and a raised eyebrow from James as if questioning me to see if I was sure.

Reluctantly I nodded. I was probably passing up the *'sperience* of a lifetime I thought as I unlocked my door and stepped inside. Then I chuckled. I'd had my first and probably only chance of what could have been a ménage à trois . . . and it wasn't so out of the question, not at all. My body thrummed with the concept . . . the possibilities. *Brick had better appreciate my sacrifice.*

I was on the top step when a fist connected with my jaw and because I was off balance the force sent me backward against the door, popping it open again. I fell out of the RV and onto the ground hitting my head on the doorframe on my way down. The side of my face was cushioned by the mat I had placed there, but I could still feel the contact my head made with the concrete pavement.

Chapter Seventeen

Jared screwed up. If he'd let me lock the door behind me before hitting me, the Johnson twins would not have pummeled him to a pulp. As it was I had to take turns pulling first one and then the other off of him.

By the time my screams alerted the neighbors and they called the police, Jared was bloody, floppy like a Raggedy Ann doll, and totally incoherent with his mumblings. He had a split eyebrow, two teeth were missing, his shoulder hung at an odd level and of course his face was a kaleidoscope of color. One kneecap was obviously paining him and he was holding his ribs as if trying to keep them in place. Two knights on white chargers had come to my rescue and done a considerable amount of damage before I could stop them.

The news of a well-known jeweler imprisoning and abusing his wife had made national headlines but the impact of the story had only been felt in the Washington metropolitan area. The news flurry had flared then died quickly. This would revive the sad story of my marriage, taking my plight nationwide yet again. I cringed at the thought. I had just gotten back into my own little world.

But by morning, news that the man who had stalked his

wife and then held her captive for ten days, and had somehow managed to fabricate a device that altered the radio signal on his ankle monitor was all over the morning talk shows. Women's rights activists were enraged that he had been released in the first place and law enforcement experts were left trying to defend the security of the system. Jared was a techno wizard, a veritable genius in gadgetry and despite my telling everyone this repeatedly, they'd ignored me. They were now going to take the proper precautionary measures. As soon as Jared was released from the hospital in Tulsa he would be extradited to Virginia and sent to a correctional facility until the trial date. Reporters were on my doorstep . . . and Brick was on the phone.

"Two thoughts," he said as I looked out the window and watched two Kansas state troopers scatter the crowd that was milling around my campsite waiting for me to emerge.

"One is you need a guard dog, I've a good mind to call my friend Wayne Simanovich and request one of his German Shepherds, and the other is, what were you doing coming home from a date with *two* men? I promised myself not to jump to conclusions this time, but really Jen, this isn't looking all that good for us."

"I can explain . . . ," I said as the troopers approached my door and knocked. I dropped the blind I was holding and went to let them in.

"Oh I'm sure you can. How about starting."

"There are state troopers at the door."

"They are there by my order. Let them in."

"Are you going to call me back?"

"No. You're going to let them in and explain what happened—to all of us. Put the speakerphone on."

I did as he said and opened the door. After introductions I invited them to sit and I went over everything the same as I had several times during the night. But there was no hope for it; the story didn't work unless I told them everything. I downplayed the kiss, made the proposition as straightforward as I could, considering how embarrassed I was with Brick on the line listening. I made sure to stress how gentlemanly both Jesse and James had been at my refusal, reiterating that the reason I was deferring was because of my strong feelings for someone else.

I didn't need to underscore that the person I was referring to was being included in this conversation. Cop-type guys have a sixth sense and seem to know the proprieties in these things. They knew damned well that the man on the other end of the phone had a vested interest in me and that he was also in a position to pull some strings for me if need be.

"So . . . you see . . . I was just having some fun, learning how to line dance and then when these guys walked me home, I was taken a little off guard by their advances. But not for one single second did I consider what they were offering. Okay, okay, maybe I did consider it for a second . . . I mean really, they are great looking guys. But it was no more than a guy would do. Scarlett Johansson walks by and you're going to consider it." I looked at the two officers—one shrugged, the other smiled.

"Jared must've been looking through the blinds during the *very few* seconds I was being held between them because I no sooner got the door open and moved up the steps, pulling the door to, when ka-pow. Fortunately I was off balance on a step and my jaw didn't have to take the force of his punch, but I did end up falling backward, which popped the door open. Luckily my hand found purchase on the doorframe for a few seconds, which gave Jesse, I think it was Jesse, time to turn and halfway catch me. And that's all she wrote.

"When the twins realized Jared had hit me, it was a free-for-all. I was lucky to finally pull them away from him. But he looked really bad. Really bad."

There was silence for about ten seconds. I looked at the cops, they looked at me, and then we all looked at the phone sitting on my knee.

"So nothing happened?" Brick's investigator voice broke the silence.

"Well yeah, something happened. Jared got the crap beat out of him."

"I mean, nothing happened between you and the Doublemints?"

I smiled at his euphemism. "No, nothing happened. Nothing would have happened. I was just surprised, never having been double-teamed like that. I was just stymied for a few minutes, trying to catch my breath . . . imagining how the hell these things worked."

"Officers? Do you need anything else?" It was obvious he wanted some alone time with me.

They both stood. One shook his head the other leaned over and spoke into the phone. "Uh, no, we got Ms. Jameson's statement last night. Seems to be the same in the retelling. The Johnson boys said pretty much the same thing. They don't have a habit of doin' this type of thing, but neither is remorseful in the least. From all we're hearing this is a man that needs putting down, or at least away."

"Yeah. This time we'd better see to it," Brick said, some of that remorse in his own voice. "Well thank you for coming out. Can you make sure she gets on her way without incident?"

"Sure thing."

They let themselves out and I switched the phone off speaker mode.

"Jenny?"

"Yeah?"

"I'm sorry."

"Not your fault."

"I told you not to worry. I said he'd be put away."

"You're not judge and jury."

"I'm supposed to be protecting you. He could have killed you." His voice was noticeably gruff. "God Jenny, I'm so sorry."

"It's okay. We're okay. Right?"

"Oh, baby, I was so worried when I got the news. You can't know. If I wasn't so damn far away, I'd be there right now."

"You can't keep leaving your job to save me."

"Then stop getting into trouble!"

I laughed. "I was just walking around the park, listening to some music, learning how to line dance . . . just trying to fit in, have some fun . . ."

"Yeah well, next time, pick some ugly guys. I saw a picture of these guys on CNN . . ."

"You're better looking."

"Really?"

"Really."

"I'm only one."

"One's all I need."

"Good."

"I've got to get going. I'm holding these troopers up, they must have better things to do than look after me."

"Honey, there is no better assignment than looking after you. You get goin' now, drive safe and I'll see you soon."

"Okay, will do."

"And Jenny?"

"Yes?"

"I love you."

I stood staring at the blank screen of my phone. He'd disconnected. I wondered idly if it was because he couldn't handle the rejection caused by me not repeating his sentiment or because he'd regretted making it.

Chapter Eighteen

It was time to get moving, getting across Kansas was going to take the better part of the day. The troopers watched and even offered to help me tear down, but I had a system and it worked for me so I declined. It had taken time for me to make doing and undoing the hooking up process efficient—streamlining the chore by wearing gloves, learning to do things in a more logical order, and figuring out that by coiling and uncoiling the hoses and cords from the bottom up that I only used what I needed and so didn't have to waste time putting things away. I was getting really good at backing up and could often come within a few feet of the electric post, faucet, or sewer connection. The confidence I had using my mirrors and the rear view camera amazed me at times.

The troopers allowed people to pass by and gape, but kept anyone from coming onto my property. They explained that as long as I rented this campsite, they could keep people from trespassing, but that at eleven, unless I opted for another day, they had no protocol to keep them from approaching me. I couldn't see why they would want to, but apparently making the national news for any reason made people manic. Quite a few people took my picture and a few women even hollered words of support.

Just as I was pulling in the slide and lifting the jacks, James and Jesse stopped by to wish me luck and to tell me they were glad they were on hand to help out last night. Of course, they now knew the whole sordid story and understood why I hadn't been interested in their proposition. They didn't seem at all concerned about the legal tussles they could be in for. I assured them that the next time I was in Kansas that I would look them up. Each one hugged me, and Jesse, who I definitely considered the friendlier of the two, patted my ass.

Minutes later I was on my way west, tapping my feet to the country music on the radio. A lot of the songs were ones I had danced to last night and my feet tapped in time to the music while I mentally did the steps in my head. I had really enjoyed learning to line dance and I promised myself that from now on I would make the effort to go to some of the classes offered at the campgrounds.

Around three, I felt I needed a break from the monotony of wheat field after wheat field, water tower after water tower— so I took a detour after seeing an interesting billboard. It would take me a total of forty miles out of my way, but I was pretty sure I would never pass this way again if it could be helped—it was just too desolate.

The home where the buffalo once roamed, with skies so vast you felt insignificant, was too far off the beaten path for me. So I thought I might as well see the world's largest ball of twine while I was so close to it. I came off Interstate 70 at Route 281 and instead of heading west I made my way east to Cawker City, where under a pavilion I learned all about Frank Stoeber's curious folly. Starting in 1953, he began winding the sisal twine from hay bales into a ball. It turned out to be a habit that was hard to break. Now bigger than a truck it's said to contain almost eight million feet of twine, weighing close to nine tons.

I was duly impressed but more so with the ingenuity of this rural town whose marketing philosophy was: given lemons make lemonade. Storefronts were painted with easily recognized icons depicted holding a ball of twine in the appropriate places: the Statue of Liberty with a twine ball for a torch, Mona Lisa holding the obsequious orb, Michelangelo's David covering his anatomic balls with a ball of twine, and Grant Wood's *American Gothic* with its depiction of a grim-faced couple spearing twine balls with their pitchfork. In an area of the country where they truly don't have much to boast about in the way of entertainment, they've made the most of a simple diversion, and I fell for it.

But they were not going to get me to drive another twenty miles north to Lebanon, the Geographic Center of the Conterminous U.S. Grabbing a handful of travel folders from a rack while walking back to my RV, I *was* disappointed that I had not known about the Oz Museum in Wamego, just a thumb's width on the map from where I'd been just last night at the campground near Topeka. No way was I backtracking, no matter how cool it sounded. I still had a somewhat serious timetable to deal with.

An hour later I was back on Route 24, heading west this time, after having had a dinner of spaghetti and apple pie at Ladow's Market, one of the many ma and pa-type diners that has outstanding food at ridiculously low prices. I was back on the road looking out at the cornflower blue sky with its wispy threads of cottony white clouds that seemed to go on forever. I was a little over halfway through Kansas and I clearly could not see a good reason why Dorothy'd had such an overwhelming desire to come back to Kansas from Oz. It was certainly not to see square strawberry rhubarb pie, a stuffed horse named Comanche, or a dead man seemingly admiring himself in a coffin. Would crossing the border into Nebraska yield anything better?

Chapter Nineteen

Having met my goal of getting into Nebraska I began scouting out a place to spend the night. I was looking for no frills and I found it in Kearney. Buffalo County Fairgrounds fit the bill perfectly. A big open area that was basically a gravel parking lot with utility poles spaced widely apart, it was a place to park and rest for the next leg of my trip. It was only ten dollars for a site that included a hook-up to an electric pole offering 50, 30 and even 20 amp connections. And there was a free dump station alongside a white picket fence. Dry camping was free with no limit for the stay. How sweet was that? Pulling onto the huge parking grid, you chose your own site and either plugged in or boondocked. It looked like they could accommodate any size rig. These people were capitalizing on what otherwise would have been just a huge, desolate parking lot.

You walked to the office to pay only if you were going to be using the power pole. If you absolutely had to have a water hook up there were two sites on the grass under some big trees. This was as accommodating as anything I'd seen for the price. Apparently they had often had a lot of people in Kearney going to the Nebraska Firefighter Museum and Education Center, the Great Platte River Road Archway Museum, the Trails and Rails

Museum, or Fort Kearney. All I needed was a place to lay my head. Which I did, almost to the minute I got back inside the Dolphin after plugging into the electric box for 30 amp service on the 6-way post.

At four in the morning another anxiety episode woke me bolt upright. My first thoughts were of Brick and his sister, Jillie, and what would happen if I screwed up this opportunity to find her. It was a given that our relationship would never be the same. Even though he'd said he loved me, there were few blossoming love affairs that could survive this kind of betrayal. Not for the first time, I wondered if I was making a huge mistake by not telling him of my plans. I paced around the quiet RV. If this wasn't lonely, I didn't know what was. There wasn't so much as an owl hooting. Who would have thought I'd miss the highway noises.

I decided that my resolution to tell my sister might have an impact on my guilt and anxiety if I would just get on the phone and call her. I looked at my cell phone now plugged into its charger on the little bar countertop behind the breakfast nook. It was too early to call and too late to take anything to get me back to sleep. I put my brown yoga pants on and added a little blue cropped spandex top and got to work: Setu Bandha Sarvangasana to calm the brain and heal tired legs; Halasana for back pain and my current insomnia; Ananda Balasana for massaging the hips; Salambhasana to stimulate the lumbar area and tone the arms and legs; Marjayasana to stretch the spinal column and contract the midriff muscles; Malasan for back and ankles and to make me think of Brick; Pigeon to build flexibility and make me feel good about what my body can do; Dolphin, for my neck, shoulders, legs, arms and feet, and finally Savasana for relaxation.

Done right, my body feels svelte, and loose, as if I could bend any which way and come back to a perfectly tall and erect posture, fully stretched with effortless ease from just about any contortion. The mind-bending effects are as beneficial as the body bending for me. A regimen of nine or ten poses always clears my mind and gives me a sense of well being, and considering I'd woken with angst and dread from a sound sleep, I knew I needed to take care of this stress or suffer through more headaches. I didn't have the time to be incapacitated, so I promised myself I would be more stringent about scheduling regular exercise— especially now when so much was at stake.

At eight thirty I called my sister. Mindful of the time difference, I knew she'd be up and getting ready for work. She was delighted to hear from me and I could actually hear her slowing down the start of her busy day to take the time to talk. After the hi-how-are-you-doing chitchat, I told her of my plans. She listened carefully and after hemming and hawing, advised me to tell Brick. She had serious concerns about me going solo on this, warning me of the dangerous position I would be putting myself in and giving me the impression that she had no confidence whatsoever in my subterfuge skills.

"I think you're going to either get hurt, get her hurt, or end up in jail. What if you kidnap a kid that really belongs to those people, supposing you can even find them to begin with?"

"I have a really good picture of Jillie taken just a few days before she was taken and I also have an age progression showing what she'd look like today."

"Those things are just supposition, you can't be sure."

"I won't take her unless I'm sure. Do you think I want to be arrested for kidnapping?"

"What I don't understand is why you can't let Brick know what you're going to be up to."

"Gloria, he's had so many bad leads and wild goose chases that even though he'd check it out as he does all the others, it would mean time away from the other important work he's doing right now. And it would just devastate me to see him disappointed again, it's easier if he doesn't even know."

"You're doing what you always try to do, the thing that keeps getting you into trouble, over and over again."

"Yeah, and what's that?"

"You're people pleasing."

"What?" I held the phone from my face and felt my face scrunch in consternation. "What are you talking about?"

"You're always trying to make other people happy, often to your own detriment."

"I do not get what you are trying to say. I think you'd better spell it out. Slowly."

"You bend over backwards to make things work out for everyone. You step in the middle of a fight and try to make everyone friends again. You hear someone say they want a red cashew nut and then you break your neck trying to find one for them."

"I don't think there is such a thing as a red cashew nut."

"That was just an example. Remember in tenth grade when your teacher lost her camera on that field trip you took to D.C. and you spent the whole next day backtracking every single place she'd been?"

"I found it, didn't I?"

"And she really appreciated it didn't she?"

"Not so much."

"Because she knew it was broken. It was easier and cheaper for her if everyone else got duplicates of their pictures and shared them with her."

"That was one case."

"One time in many. When you were dating Jared you did every single thing in your power to make him appreciate you. He didn't even *have* to court you, or give chase, you fell right at his feet."

"That was not a simple case of people pleasing, I was in love with him."

"Yeah, well . . . you see where that got you. I'm just saying . . . you do not have to make everyone's world perfect. Especially in this case. You could really screw things up this time."

"Listen, I only called because I wanted someone to know what I was up to in case things go flooey. In the event, my *people-pleasing little ol' self* makes some kind of mistake. So, despite my well-meaning intentions, if I do end up in trouble, or God forbid, these people figure out what I'm up to, will you please call Brick and fill him in?"

"And exactly how will I know to do this?"

"I'll call you at about this time every day just to check in. If you don't hear from me by, say, ten o'clock every morning then I want you to call Brick and tell him what I was up to. Can you do that? Do you think you can possibly overlook my over zealous people-pleasing tendencies one more time, and let me see if I can do this one thing right?"

"Yeah. Sure," she said with obvious reluctance. "Let me get this straight: you call every morning, so I don't have to—you don't call, and I have to get reinforcements as you're likely to be tied up in a closet somewhere."

"Yeah, something like that. But the thing is, you're not calling to get me rescued, you're calling so Brick doesn't lose this opportunity to find his sister. That's the important thing, letting him know what I've discovered about her."

"See, people-pleasing . . . you want him happy, and you're not even thinking about what could happen to you."

"Isn't that what you do when you care about people?"

"You care about this guy that way?"

"What way?"

"You know what way. The same way you cared about Jared when you married him. You cared about him so much that you did everything he said and ignored everything we said. He convinced you that your family didn't matter, that only he did. He made you give up everything you cared about so you could focus solely on him."

"You can't seriously believe I'm dumb enough to let any man come between me and my family again, do you?"

"Well, I would hope not. But you do have that people-pleasing thing going on, and I know how you get . . ."

"Trust me, I am not going to ever sacrifice my happiness for a man's . . . any man's."

"Well that's good to hear."

"But I would really love it if I could pull this off. Gosh, the look on his face when he sees his sister . . . it's what I think about and dream about."

"See?"

"Okay. Maybe you're right. I do want to please him. But who wouldn't? He's a wonderful man who I care about."

"Do you love him?"

I thought for a few moments before answering. "I don't know. I know I love being with him. And he's all I think about when he's gone. But I don't know. I kind of like being independent right now and I don't want anyone I have to answer to."

"That's understandable after all you've been through. Speaking of which, I saw your picture on the news again."

"I know, apparently it's a slow news week."

"Have you spoken with your attorney?"

"Oh yeah, many times."

"And what's he saying?"

"That he wants to go for more alimony and for half the franchises."

"Don't you think you deserve that?"

"I just want to be free of him. If I make him pay through the nose, it's only going to come back on me. I know that in my bones."

"Sounds like you need a hit man."

"I had two of them and I made them stop."

"See? People-pleasing again. What were you thinkin'? Were you tryin' to keep your lawyer happy? You know he would have been crying his eyes out if those guys had kept at it until Jared breathed his last breath."

"I don't know what I was thinking. I just knew I couldn't

let them kill him."

"Well listen, if you really want to please me, *and* mom and dad, next time someone is in a position to take Jared out, let 'em. That would please *me* greatly."

"I'll keep that in mind. Meanwhile . . ."

"Meanwhile . . . give me Brick's number."

I gave her all the contact information I had for Brick Tyler, thanked her, and then told her I loved her. Then I made myself a bowl of oatmeal and headed out. Nebraska, Wyoming, Utah, Idaho, and Oregon—in their turn—awaited me.

Chapter Twenty

I was on Route 80 heading west and according to my little G.P.S., that I didn't trust so much, I would have the pleasure of being on this road for another 688 miles—all of Nebraska and partway through Wyoming. It would be two days before I reached Route 84, and about an inch northeast of Salt Lake City according to my map, which I figured to be close to thirty miles as the crow flies. I was not looking forward to this part of the journey. I thought it might be boring. I was right.

Everything interesting was north of where I was, even "Carhenge," a ring of vintage cars painted gray and sunk part way into the ground, was too far north to consider detouring. The Druidic "stones" of Alliance, Nebraska could possibly be on the agenda for the return trip, I told myself as I sat in my Dolphin at a rest stop, maps and brochures spread out over the table and the seats.

After a quick nap, I folded everything up and hopped back into the driver's seat. I was halfway through Stieg Larsson's *The Girl with the Dragon Tattoo* so I was being entertained, just not so much by the vista anymore. Although I had seen some lovely purple flowers peeking out from stony outcroppings here and there, and some moss-covered retaining walls that looked like they'd been there for centuries. They blended into the landscape so well that on meandering roads I was just about past them before I spotted them. I made it to Cheyenne with minimal effort and as I wasn't really all that tired, I decided to try for Laramie. Huge mistake.

The campground in Laramie was disappointing to say the least. The gravel road was lumpy and uneven. Even with my jacks lowered I wasn't able to get the Dolphin level and the noise, oh my gosh, it was so loud. The price you pay for staying close to an Interstate I told myself, and searched in the cabinet beside the sink for my box of disposable earplugs. There was no way I was going to be able to watch TV so after a quick dinner of tomato soup and a grilled cheese sandwich, I relaxed in the tub with one of my romance novels. I'd had enough of trying to keep track of all the characters in the Stieg Larsson book and was taking a break with something frivolous where the only people I had to keep track of were the hero and heroine. Sadly, that left me missing Brick even more. I decided I'd email him.

Not having the reliable Internet connection that was advertised in the flyer, I made my way to the office only to discover no one there. When I got back to my RV, I found my phone and punched in Brick's number.

"Wondering when I'd hear from you," he said in a deep throaty voice.

"Makin' my way west, takin' my time," which was so not true, "and lovin' life."

"Don't tell me, you found a set of triplets." I could hear his smile.

"I don't think I have enough body parts to keep a set of triplets satisfied," I teased.

"Trust me. You do."

"Hmmm. I should probably Google the next triplet convention, see where it is."

"You should Google 'Ways Cops have of restraining naughty girls.'"

"I already know how they do that."

"Do ya now?" I loved the way a brogue softened his voice when he was intrigued.

"Silk ties, long boas, handcuffs . . . you have any of them handy?"

"I might be able to scare up a pair of handcuffs, maybe even a blindfold."

"Would be nice if you could just beam yourself here."

"Where might here be?"

"Laramie, Wyoming."

"Ugh. Not the prettiest part of the state."

"I know, and this campground doesn't have a lot going for it. I should have stopped in Cheyenne."

"Why didn't you?"

"Just wasn't all that tired, wanted to push on."

"Why? What's your hurry?"

I knew I had screwed up as soon as I said it. "No hurry really. Just got in a groove, had a book on CD in the player, and was hoping I could find a lovely little park to sip some merlot."

"You're too far south, everything of any consequence is farther north—The Grand Tetons, National Elk Preserve, Yellowstone, Cody, Jackson, even Thermopolis is north of where you are."

"Thermopolis?"

"The Wyoming Dinosaur Center."

"Oh. I'm really sorry to be missing that . . ."

"If I was close I'd take you to the Mural Room Breakfast Buffet at the Jackson Lake Lodge, a view to die for and a full breakfast bar where I could replenish my body after exhausting myself in your bed."

"What, no helicopter?"

"I'm in D.C."

"D.C.? What are you doing there?"

"Speaking at a conference on Internet chat rooms."

"Don't you ever get tired of all the travel?"

"Not the camping type, but I sure do hate all this commercial flying. It used to be fun a few years back, but traveling as I do is a grind."

"The airlines used to be more accommodating."

"Speaking of which, you told me once that you'd never flown, that time I was trying to get you to fly with me to Utah with Angelina. Then later I found out that you'd flown from Virginia to North Carolina to buy your first RV, and then you flew back to Virginia from Austin when Jared managed to surprise you at the house. Why did you lie to me about never having flown?"

"You mean when we were outside of Shreveport?"

"Yeah."

"I was afraid."

"Of what?"

"Being on my own in Utah, without my home, with a little girl in tow. My motorhome is my security now not just my home, I didn't want to leave it behind. "

"I was going to go with you."

"You always leave me."

There was silence on the line.

"Yeah, I always do, don't I?"

"Yeah." My voice was childlike and I heard the longing in it.

"I'm going to have to work on that. But still you lied to me."

"I know. I'm afraid you're going to have to punish me." This time I adopted a mulish, pouty voice, just to tease him.

I could hear his breath hitch. "Mmm . . . what did you have in mind?"

"I suppose I'll have to *submit* to your desires. Maybe stand in the corner or kneel at your feet . . ."

Again . . . that husky, sharp intake. "Jenny, why are you doing this to me when I'm clear across the country? Jesus, I'm as hard as an iron pike."

"Save it."

"Save it? I can't stand in front of hundreds of police officers talking about online perverts with a pole tenting my trousers like this."

"Stand behind the podium."

"I'll tell you what I'm going to stand behind . . ."

"Promises, promises . . ."

"Jenny, next time I see you, you'd better not bend over in my presence."

"Or what?"

"My poker will be poking you that's what!"

"I will be so looking forward to that," I laughed and then made some kissy noises. "Night Lover."

"Night!" he said with a gruff voice. I was thrilled I had him hot and bothered.

I read for a little while, my ears stuffed with soft lime green plugs to drown out the noise of the Interstate. I was on my second glass of wine when I thought I heard my phone ring. I didn't get to it in time, but the beep indicated there was a message on my voice mail.

Chapter Twenty-one

At first, I couldn't make out the voice, what was being said or who it belonged to. Then my body stiffened as I realized it was Jared who had left the message.

My attorney had told me he was back in the D.C. area, in a rehab facility that housed criminals who had either broken parole or violated terms of their house arrest. He'd had to have his jaw wired shut and that's why I couldn't understand the muffled, garbled rantings—until I had played it over a few times.

"Think you're so smart," "I hear you're having fun screwing every man in sight," "Don't think this is over," "Next time your ass is going to be rammed with a cannon," "You and all your boyfriends are going to pay for this," "Mark my words, we are *not* over," "You belong to me, you promised yourself to me and I'm going to make you honor that promise," "Believe me, this pain I'm in will not go unpunished."

When the prompts came on asking if I wanted to save or delete the message, I stored it. I would have to send it to my attorney's cell phone tomorrow. I could not believe Jared was being stupid enough to allow himself to be recorded threatening me like that. I closed the phone and plugged it back into the charger. How had he gotten the number this time? I had a fairly new phone, only a few weeks old. The no-contract-no-statement type, the ones you bought prepaid minutes for. Very few people had the number: my sister and my parents, Daniel, his wife Julie and their daughter Angelina, my attorney, Brick, and of course, Randy. Diana had it, but her new husband, Connor, did not as he was overseas now. None of those people would have been careless with it.

I thought back to when I had given each person the number and realized with sudden dread, that in each instance, I had passed the number on by email. He wouldn't . . . He couldn't . . . . But I knew he could. He hacked into my email account! There was no other way he could have gotten the number this time. I had been careful, very careful.

What else could he know? I went over to my laptop and clicked on the icon for my email account and was surprised when the connection went through. Before I could scroll through the sent messages I heard the telltale ping of an incoming message. I clicked to see who would be emailing me at this time of night and saw only a subject line saying Wedding pictures. Thinking it might be from Diana, I clicked on it. It wasn't from Diana.

A picture of Jared and I posing for the camera after saying our vows opened on the screen—filling it. I focused on the starry-eyed ingénue looking back at me. I looked so happy. Then I stared at Jared, he had been so handsome, so perfect. I had felt as lucky as any bride that I was standing beside him walking down the aisle as his wife. What had happened? Shaking my head, I unconsciously scrolled down and a second picture opened on screen. I jumped back from the disgusting sight. A much beaten up Jared, sat naked in a chair his hand gripping his erect penis. Even though his jaw was wired, he'd managed to leer for the camera. And heaven help me, I stupidly scrolled further down to see a mock up picture of me, kneeling at his feet, my head bent, appearing as if I was getting ready to suck his penis. I recognized the picture as one taken at the reception when I'd been placing my garter on his thigh. It had been a playful gesture then, it was a vile one now, but what made the picture so evil was the look on his face. He had the light of a demented entity in his eyes—a fiend gone mad. My husband, the man I had vowed to cherish and love forever, had absolutely lost his mind. Nothing could make it any clearer and I had to wonder at the stupidity of him giving me this much ammunition. My attorney would be getting a big fat pay check for a job that would now consist of not much more than filling out some papers for the court.

With the amount of money involved, and no pre-nup, I had been advised to hire a team of attorneys; a local firm that specialized in representing wealthy socialites in the D.C. area had actually come to my hospital room at my father's request. Instead, budgetary reasons not withstanding, I chose a husband and wife team who specialized in divorce cases for battered spouses. I had read about them years ago in the *Washington Post Magazine*, never dreaming I'd ever need them, but impressed, I remembered their names.

I sighed and closed my email program and shut my computer down. I would deal with all this tomorrow. In the meantime, I thought I would add a little more wine to make my melancholy complete. After another glass of merlot I decided to call my drinking buddy in Pahrump, Nevada.

Chapter Twenty-two

"Not too many people can track me down at the tables, honey," Craig said. I could hear the noise of the casino in the background. "I don't answer this phone for anybody when I got a stack of chips runnin' through ma fingers. But you know you're special," his gruff voice softened, "what's up?"

Just hearing his Texas drawl cheered me, but still my voice came out on a sob, "I needed to hear your voice."

"That's nice to hear. Thought you'd forgotten all about me."

"Never. You're the unforgettable type."

"Wish I'd been the weddible type. What's that I hear in your voice, you cryin'?"

"No not really. Or at least not yet."

I could hear the background noise lessening as if he was either shielding the phone or walking away from the action.

"How 'bout you tell me what's botherin' ya. I'll get me a box of chocolates and a jug o'wine and it'll be just like ol' times. We'll talk into the night."

And that's exactly what we did. Around four o'clock we signed off, promising to keep in touch more often and agreeing that we'd hook up on my return trip. I did not tell him why I was going to Oregon. I didn't need another man trying to talk me out of things I wanted to do, and Craig, as protective as he was of me, would surely have a fit if he knew what I was planning.

Ever since he and his chauffeur rescued me when my RV overheated in Death Valley he'd been a good friend. He wanted to be more, but understood that it wasn't what I wanted. He was the epitome of a gentleman, and more fun than wallowing in the mud. We'd actually watched a porn move together in one of the rooms in the hotel he owned in Pahrump and had laughed ourselves silly while polishing off vintage bottles of wine. I trusted him like a brother.

I fell asleep and for the first time ever, almost didn't make checkout time. I pulled up by the office and "stole" their wireless connection long enough to send a message to my attorneys, forwarding the pictures Jared had sent to both them and to Brick.

I shouldn't have been surprised when not an hour later, while I was making my way through Medicine Bow National Forest, my cell phone rang.

"What a pretty little bride you were. Shame you married such a jerk."

"I was kinda cute, wasn't I?"

"You were gorgeous, still are."

"Thank you. Any other comments?"

"I like the position you were in on the last one, just not your focal point. He's going to a lot of trouble to impress. Can't help but wonder what his game is. Hey, is he bigger than me, kinda looks it from this angle."

I had to laugh. With everything we were dealing with, his concern was that I might be comparing and finding him lacking. "Trust me, McCoy is the perfect size. I like all of your parts better than any of his, especially your mind. I think he's lost it—one too many blows to the head. I wonder if he realizes how easy he's making all the legal stuff for me."

"Yeah, his attorney is going to have a fit when he

sees this."

"I already sent it to mine."

"Sending porn on the Internet? I could have you arrested you know . . ."

"It's not kiddie porn, so no, you cannot."

"Speaking of which, I have to skedaddle. I'm on in twenty minutes and I need another cup of coffee to smooth out my voice. I think I woke up with a cold."

"It's probably just Washington allergies, I sure don't miss them."

"Travel safe. Next time send me a picture of you naked. My memory is fadin'."

"Not a chance. You can refresh your memory in a few weeks."

"Good-bye sexy."

"Take care of McCoy."

"I always do."

Chapter Twenty-three

After a desperate search for a much needed latte, I finally pulled into a parking lot that bordered a McDonald's. I didn't do fast food often, but for some reason a Quarter Pounder and a vanilla latte appealed to me. It was time for a break and I needed to start planning a campground for tonight. I had made Evanston okay, now my goal was Ogden, in Utah.

I consulted one of my campground directories and decided on East Canyon Resort, just south of Henefer because it was away from the highway and according to my atlas, East Canyon was a state park. I was ready for something lovely to look at after Laramie. So, latte in hand, I climbed back into my RV and followed the directions after plugging in the address on my G.P.S. unit. I called her Gypsy because she was quite the wanderer; I'd learned that she was not always prone to picking the most direct route. But she was company on an otherwise tedious trip. Sometimes I changed her voice and made her British when American Gypsy began to annoy me.

It was lovely, rocky outcroppings everywhere, sheer walls of amber rock placed by the hand of God as if he'd been on hands and knees playing a game, moving them about for esthetic appeal. Despite the general impression of a desert, there were plenty of trees, cedar in particular, and lots of green shrubbery scattered here and there. The mountains reminded me of a backdrop for a western and I could just picture cowboys on fleet-footed roans. I happily pulled in and began setting up house. I had no idea I was in dirt bike and ATV heaven until dinnertime.

It seemed as if on cue, scores of bikes revved up and sped away. Their engines could be heard for many miles as they chased each other back and forth and up and down making dusty paths.

Thankfully, as dusk settled in they all came home to roost and I could hear myself think again. I sat outside enjoying the noises of the night until I felt the bugs zeroing in, then I went inside to watch some TV. I loved watching nature shows that featured this part of the country. I was very eager to learn about each area I was in. Utah, I knew was particularly beautiful, especially in the area that skirts around the Great Salt Lake. I was surprised that there was a Dolphin Island at the northern end, which I wouldn't be going anywhere near. At 4200 feet above sea level, the lake was an oddity. Due to the shallowness the total area fluctuated between a low of 950 square miles to a high of 3300. I wondered how they figured the setbacks for building in this area.

I was nodding off during the late news so I took myself off to bed with the hopes of sleeping in the next morning and having a nice leisurely breakfast before getting back on the road. This morning's harried tear down had not started my day off in the best way. Of course, the wine from the night before could have had a bit to do with that, too, I told myself as I washed my face, slipped on a nightgown and fell between the sheets.

I woke with a start sitting bolt upright, grabbing the sheets to my chest and turning my head this way and that trying to figure out where all the noise was coming from. It was as if I was in the center of a wagon train being circled by Indians on dirt bikes. I looked at the digital clock velcroed to my nightstand.

Six a.m. I moaned and fell back on the bed. The denizens on dirt bikes and ATVs were at it again. No sooner had the sun made itself known than these guys came out to chase it. Vvvrroom, vrrooom, rawrr, and raaawrr, pop-pop-pop-pop-pop filled the air as engines strained, throated down and then backfired. Over and over again. I heard each bike cycle, wheeze, sputter and then catch and soar as their riders raced and teased each other. I threw the sheets off my body. No way was I sleeping with all this noise. And no way was I going to even try to have a leisurely breakfast thinking home-home-on-the-range thoughts. I dressed and got my own little bike off the back and went looking for a nice place to have breakfast.

With the help of two elderly gentlemen I found on a street corner, I found Ruth's Diner, founded in 1930 and serving what the locals considered the best breakfast to be found. I had Ruth's Frittata, a fresh egg omelet with basil tomato and feta and a sliver of the Banana Walnut French Toast I ordered to take home to reheat later. I was careful to only put butter and cinnamon sugar on the part I was going to eat now so the rest didn't get soggy. I smiled and chatted up to the locals while I stuffed my face full of great food. Sadly, I did not end up having much French toast to take back with me, which turned out all right as I discovered I had no way to get it home on the bike anyway.

I groaned as I made my way out to the parking lot. I could not remember the last time I had eaten so much. It was actually an effort to get my leg over the bike so I could straddle it. I knew as soon as I got back to the campground I was going to have to run or walk this off, either that or succumb to carbohydrate overload and crash.

Back at the ranch—gosh I always wanted to say that, and this was the most appropriate place by far—the cowboys and Indians were still at it so I joined in and followed a few on my little Vespa until I realized how filthy I was getting. Back at the ranch--that is just so cool—I grabbed my collapsible hamper filled with dirty laundry before deciding I should add what I was wearing to the pile. I walked to the bathhouse to shower and change. Then it was off to do the weekly washing.

I jogged around the area until it was time to move things from the washer to the dryer then I sat reading my book until it was time to fold everything. I went back to my RV and as the cowboys say, broke camp. I did the final policing of my campsite before getting behind the wheel and pulling out. I would surely put Utah behind me today and begin traversing the lower quadrant of Idaho on my way to Oregon.

I still had a few days to spare, and thought maybe I would treat myself to a day off from driving tomorrow. That was if I found a nice, *quiet* campground tonight. Boise looked promising, maybe even Sun Valley, although that was a bit out of the way. I wanted to stay in a nice place tonight and I was ready to say to hell with the budget and pay double if I had to.

The skies were a soft pale blue with streaks of spun cotton stretching out across the horizon. Against the backdrop of the mountains and the barren plains it was postcard perfect. After my huge breakfast, it wasn't likely that I'd need to stop to eat until late this afternoon so Gypsy and I finished listening to my book on CD while marveling at the scenery as it whipped past the windows.

Chapter Twenty-four

I finished my book on CD and listened to some music for a while, then turned to talk radio. I was antsy. Tired of driving, but barely past Twin Falls. I needed coffee if I was going to continue on, and wireless Internet. I needed to check out a few campgrounds and this time I was going to check out RV Reviews and see what they recommended.

In Gooding I found a nice coffee shop although I had to park quite a bit away and walk to it. But once inside, I was enveloped with the wonderful smell of roasting coffee and cinnamon buns. I got my skinny latte, this time with hazelnut shots and took my laptop to a table in the corner. While I waited for it to boot up I sipped my latte and looked around. This appeared to be moose country for sure. I imagined that in the winter this was either one very empty place or the life of the city.

A man in jogging clothes came in, nodded to the barista, and smiled at me. I smiled back. He was young and athletic looking, and what any girl in her right mind would call cute, but he didn't appeal to me, not at all. I realized then that I had a one-item list of criteria for men now: hunky/sexy/cop, and that only Brick could fit that bill for me. It was as if I didn't even need to bother to look anymore. I watched the jogger bend over the counter to flirt with the girl at the register. Nice tight buns in spandex. Okay, I still needed to look.

My laptop pinged and I was taken back to the cyber world. One of my attorneys had acknowledged my email and advised me of an impending court date where it would pretty much be show and tell so everyone could plan their strategy. He said ours was straightforward and that no judge would deny our motion. He said I should be divorced by the end of the year if not sooner. I thanked him for the work he and his wife were doing on my behalf and said I'd check in with him next week.

I Googled the next big city I would come to on Route 84—Mountain Home, and added + RV campground, then hit return. I clicked on RV Park Reviews when it popped up then scrolled through the listings reading every single line. I sat back with a huge grin. Mountain Home RV Park had a 9, a 10, and another 10! I had hardly ever seen a park with one ten, and here was one rated with back-to-back tens! And as a bonus, it was a Good Sam's Park so I could get a discount. All right, home sweet home . . . at least for tonight. I read everything written on their website then called and asked if they had a site available. I was in luck as it was still early in the day so they still had a few. I asked them to hold a site for me, told them where I was now and was told it would be an hour and half before I got there. I closed my laptop and hopped up with a smile for everyone. Joggerboy obviously thought I was smiling just for him and flashed me an all-knowing grin and winked. I think he was a bit surprised when I walked right past him. As far as I was concerned, I was already spoken for, but it was always nice to know I could still catch another man's eye. I loved this life. The freedom to decide, the freedom to live each day as it came—to go, do, enjoy as things came up. Right now I was on my way to a campground that was rated a ten! After marginally enjoying several I would rate as a four or five—six at best—I was pumped.

Sure enough, an hour and half later I pulled off Interstate 84 at exit 95 and just past the Wal-Mart I found Mountain

Home RV Campground. I was immediately impressed as the immaculate park spread out before me. I was met by a friendly host who helped me select a site and checked me in. The spaces all seemed large and level which was a plus I could certainly appreciate now. The pull-throughs were concrete and had extra room to park your tow vehicle. They even had Buddy Pads so if you were traveling with friends your units could face each other. They were about the widest and longest lots I'd seen so far—I would actually be able to put out my awning if I wanted to. And there were a lot of grassy areas, along with a picnic table—which I was coming to learn, was not always a standard item.

It looked like a very nice park, exceptional, from what I'd seen so far. I knew it was convenient to some stores and restaurants, as I'd seen them when I came off the highway. Children were riding bikes on the paved roads and there was a distinct smell of floribunda roses wafting on the summer air. I felt as if I'd lucked into an RV paradise.

While I was hooking up and setting up my "front porch," awning and all, I was privileged to be able to look up and see a flyover from Mountain Home AFB, a few miles away. They were doing training flights and the sight and sounds of the powerful jets flying directly overhead both thrilled and dismayed me. I thought of Connor and all the other servicemen and women laying it on the line so I could have the freedom to move as I pleased, to enjoy this beautiful country and all its bounty.

Then as if everything else wasn't enough, I took a nice long shower and was amazed at the water pressure, it felt great on my back and neck. For the first time ever, I attached my regulator, just in case. Water pressure this high was a rarity on the road.

After dressing in shorts and a tank I flip-flopped my way around getting the lay of the land. I found the rose garden near the entrance that was responsible for the wonderful aroma. I peaked into the bathhouses and was surprised by the individual restrooms, each with its own shower, toilet, vanity sink and counter top. I practically swooned when I saw the laundry room and decided I'd have to strip the bed before I left just so I could try the sparkling machines out, it would be a shame to waste such a clean, modern laundromat. At the Library Exchange I saw a few books I might like to trade for before I left.

I bought a few postcards at the office and began walking back to my RV to fill them out. I could hear the shriek of laughter coming from kids at the playground and my nose detected the unmistakable aroma of a steak covering incinerating charcoal. My tummy made appreciating noises and I patted it. I didn't think it would settle for another PB & J sandwich or a frozen dinner. I had a skirt steak in the freezer I could thaw, and the rest of the ingredients for fajitas. I smiled as I made my way back, yeah, that's the ticket.

Dinner was exceptional if I do say so myself and I dawdled at the table picking tasty tidbits from the cast iron serving pan I had used to cook everything in. The day was winding down and the sunset, just off to the right, promised to be spectacular. The only thing missing was . . . well, clearly for me it was a man— one very special and very desired man.

I mentally sifted through my battery drawer, the one under the fridge, just off the floor. I wondered if I had enough batteries to replenish my little "silver bullet." Originally a gag gift when my girlfriends threw a going away party for me when I left work and married Jared, I had held onto it for sentimental reasons. They'd mischievously had it engraved with my initials. While packing to leave Virginia and Jared, I had come across it and thrown it into my backpack. It had quickly become indispensable, literally my best friend at hand. I'd even had to replace the batteries—twice. I smiled at the thought of that awkward moment. I'd had to surreptiously open it in the store to see what kind of batteries it took, as they were the flat hearing-aid type. The saleslady saw me, recognized what it was, laughed and handed me the package I needed. I'd asked for the larger, economy size, so I'd have spares. Now what had I done with them?

Fireworks lit the sky in an area southwest of where the park was and I wondered if they were coming from the Air Force Base. Then I cleared the table in anticipation of creating my own individual fireworks. I wondered if Brick was taking matters into his own hand on this beautiful summer night too. He would still be in D.C., probably getting ready to go out to dinner with colleagues. Attractive agents like Vanessa came to mind.

But I didn't worry about him, just as I hoped he didn't worry about me. Things would work out for us, of that I had no doubt. I was willing to wait. Hell, when I thought about my life on the road, I couldn't believe how relatively short it had been considering all I had done and the people I had met. By rights, I should still be mourning the death of my marriage, not anticipating a life on the road with Brick. But my marriage had died years ago, it had just taken a few years to get the courage to walk way—okay . . . run away.

A family walked by and I was drawn to the little scene. A fair-haired boy about five was riding a bike with training wheels, the father gingerly guiding him with his hand on the back of the seat. He was wearing a golf shirt, long pants and golf shoes, and I wondered if he had spent his day at Desert Canyon Golf Course just up the road. A little girl with long blonde braids was clutching a disheveled doll baby, dragging her feet and scuffing the toes of her sneakers on the pavement as she walked beside the mother who was pushing a fancy top-of-the-line stroller. She looked tired, but happy.

I focused on the little girl because of her size and coloring. She could be mine, I thought. Easily. I realized—not for the first time—that I wanted a little miniature of me like that. The mother smiled over at me and then looked down at her daughter and smiled at her while she answered a question. I wanted what she had, I thought. I want that man, that little girl, and possibly that little boy, too. But not the stroller, definitely not the stroller. It was too ostentatious; I would be more the papoose carrying type, one of those organic ladies who were into natural childbirth who carried their babies swaddled in a sling at their breasts.

Breasts . . . that made me think of a baby nursing. Then my mind segued to Brick's lips sucking and tugging and I tripped going up the steps leading into my RV. Well tonight I might get some kind of satisfaction on my own, but without the man of my dreams in my arms, covering my body with his, I certainly wouldn't be starting that family.

The next day I woke to a bright sunny day and set off to do some sightseeing. Sometime during the night I confirmed my earlier decision to treat myself and stay an extra day. I was told there were plenty of restaurants and shops to browse through and quite a few outfitters in the area that could set me up for just about any sport. So I spent the day riding my Vespa and enjoying the sights. Driving by the scenic overpasses I saw people fishing the Snake River and the South Fork of the Boise River. It looked to be a grand day and everyone was reveling in it.

I found a nice deli to buy an Italian sub and took a bottle of water from my saddlebag. Then I sat on the edge of a fountain enjoying the cooling mist from the water hitting the rocks at my back. I couldn't remember being at peace like this. It was lovely having no place to be and having no one to answer to. The longing I'd had last night for a family of my own was gone, it was as if another woman had fantasized it instead of me. I guess there were times when you wanted a part of each. Today, I wanted to just be with me.

Around three I decided it was time to head back to camp. I could feel my skin warm and tingly from the sun and knew after my shower I'd have some nice color. Looking at my gas gage I thought now would be a good time to fill up, as I never knew where I'd be next when I wanted to use the bike. I remembered seeing a gas station on the way back and pulled in behind several others who had the same idea. I stopped at the air hose first to check the tire pressure then selected a pump.

In an effort to keep track of my expenses I always use my debit card, even if it's only going to be a few bucks, which it generally was for the Vespa. While I was waiting for my card to be authorized I pulled out the receipt someone had left in the slot and almost fell out of my sandals when I saw the name printed on the receipt. *Robert W. Brynes.*

Could it possibly be? Could he have been so close? A chill went up my spine and all the joy from the day drained out. I looked at the amount on the receipt—$75. I recognized the amount as the most you could usually charge at a time at these automatic pumps. Unless it was a truck or SUV of some kind, it had to be an RV to have taken on this much gas. What were the odds? I looked around but there was no truck or RV in sight. Most of the cars at the pumps were small sedans and the ones parked right in front of the mini-mart were compacts.

I continued to stare at the receipt. Chances are he hadn't even gone inside. I noted the time, and inched my cell phone out of my front pocket. Six minutes. I had missed him by six minutes. Had Jillie been with him? Had they been staying in the area or were they just passing through on their way to The Rally? I folded the receipt and slipped it into my pocket along with my phone. The display, having timed out for my PIN, was back to welcoming me and asking me to insert my card. I pressed clear and started all over again.

The Vespa took twelve dollars. It was the first time I could remember having the pump shut off in my hand without me noticing. I blinked when it jerked in my hand. How could a day with so much promise turn so ugly so fast? How could I go from being so elated and content to being so itchy, restless and scared? The dread of all that was ahead hit me with the force of a mallet. I was suddenly drained. I didn't even know if I could make it back on the Vespa.

I replaced the nozzle and waited for my receipt. Then I snapped my helmet back in place and found the energy to lift my leg over the manifold. On autopilot, I put the key in the ignition and turned it over. The sound of the engine jolted me back to the present and I shook my head to clear it. I had a job to do. I had to get back, pack up and be ready to move out at first light. I had to find Jillie and there was no point in wasting any more time. If they were this close there was only one place they would be heading.

Chapter Twenty-five

Back at Mountain Home I went to the bathhouse and took a long, pelting shower. I hadn't ridden the Vespa like that since the last time I was out West after I'd taken Angelina back to Utah. I'd forgotten how hilly it was, which seemed to play havoc with my back even though I tried to maintain good posture, but I couldn't help being bounced around on a lot of the older roads. Still wrapped in my robe I stretched out on the sofa and took a nice long nap. It was late when I woke, the sun was setting with pale pastel streaks. I bypassed dinner for cheese and crackers that I snacked on while putting on my workout clothes then I went outside with my Yoga mat to get the kinks out of my back. I was holding Pigeon pose when the cell phone that I'd placed on the picnic table began vibrating against the planks. It was late, the sun all but set, there was only a glimmer of purple left to be snuffed out on the horizon. Who could that be, I wondered as I stood and walked over to the table.

I didn't recognize the number at first, then with surprise I realized it was Randy, the guy I'd met at Las Cruces, the man who had steered me to this rally in the first place with his phone message left while I was in the hospital in Virginia.

"Well hello, there. You gettin' everything set up?" I knew

the early bird arrival dates were July 12th and 13th, and that most vendors liked to set up a few days before in anticipation of extra sales. I was planning on getting there the morning of the 12th.

"Yeah, everything's pretty much done on my end. Hey, I thought I'd warn ya about somethin'."

"Yeah, what's that?"

"I saw this Byrnes guy, even chatted him up a bit. He just got here a little while ago. I saw him unloading all his stuff in the warehouse where the vendor's are setting up. He's a strange one all right. I told him I had some kids looking for friends to play with until the Rally opened and the programs for the kids were underway. I asked if he knew of any young kids they could play with and he said he had a daughter and maybe they could play with her, just maybe. He must keep his daughter on a tight leash. They have a whole slew of things planned for the Youth Activity Program—pizza parties, games, crafts, magic shows, puppets, even a carnival of sorts, but he says he's not sure he's going to let her do any of it. Says there's too many perverts at these things, which is so not true. I've never heard of an incident at any of the hundreds of rallies I've worked at."

"So what does this mean, will I even be able to meet this daughter? I wonder if he ever lets her out in public."

"Yeah, I actually saw her—she was helpin' her ma wash the windshield on their rig. She's cute, but she seems shy."

"So what do you suggest?"

"I don't think you're going to get close to her unless you stay with the vendors. Even though there's over three hundred of us, we're a close-knit group, most of us know each other from other rallies. There's a level of trust among the vendors, they look out for each other. Most will cover each other's booths for breaks even though they've never met before. If you could be living on site with the vendors, you'll have a much better chance of seeing this girl. If you stay in the main area with the attendees and volunteers you'll be suspect every time you wander this way."

"But how can I be a vendor? I don't have anything to sell, and I haven't even applied, surely they're filled up by now."

"No, I heard one of the workers say they have ten spots left. You can download the application and email it, I'm fairly certain they'll let you in even at this late date."

"But what will I sell?"

"I don't know. Do you make anything RVers could use? Can you demonstrate something and sell it, even if it's jewelry or pottery or some such? Kitchen items seem to go over well at these things, micro-fiber towels, special candles or soaps . . . how-to books . . ."

I thought for a moment and an idea flew into my head. "How about a camping cookbook?"

"Yeah, that would work. But what're you going to do, go buy some RV cookbooks and then resell them? I don't think there's any money in that, so you'll seem a little odd doin' that."

"How about if I sold my *own* cookbook?"

"You have your own cookbook?" His tone was incredulous.

"I've got some family recipes I've been doctoring for RVing that I've put on my laptop, I'll combine them, do some quick formatting, and get Kinko's to print a hundred copies. Will that work?"

"Hell, if it's any good, you could easily sell a thousand."

"Randy, stay on track—the idea here is not to sell books, the idea is find Jillie, verify she's Brick's daughter and find a way to rescue her."

"Yeah, got carried away there. Anyway, cookbooks would be just fine. And you'll need some kind of sign and a booth of some sort."

"A booth?"

"Just go to Wal-Mart and get one of those canopies they sell in the camping department for sixty or seventy bucks. Then all you'll need is a table and a chair to put under it. You'll also need a bank bag to make change so you'll look the part. A lot of people will be miffed you don't take charge cards, but as you said, the idea is not to sell books, the idea is to live among the vendors so you'll have the opportunity to run into this Byrnes' girl."

"Yeah. Thanks for calling Randy. I really appreciate all you're doing for me."

"Hell it's not much. Besides, if it weren't for you, I think I'd've left Charlotte by now, and that wouldn't have been good for the kids."

"How's she doing?"

"We're seeing a counselor twice a month now. She gets to yell at me and then I get to yell back. Then the doc tell us what we have to work on for the next two weeks and we go home and cuddle."

"Not making love yet though?"

"She says not until she gets the prosthetic legs. She wants to have legs instead of stumps when we do it. She's been fitted and they've been ordered. I'm anxious to see if we can get back what we had before the accident."

"You two have gone through a lot, but it's getting through the tough times that makes a marriage work." As I said that I thought of my own marriage. There was no getting through the tough times for Jared and me. He was the one responsible for the tough times, and he'd never been interested in doing anything more than continuing them. My interests didn't lie with reconciliation, they never had. Once I'd finally forged the courage to leave, I'd known that there would be no turning back.

"I wish I could hire you for my team or set you up with someone else's but if Charlotte ever got wind . . ."

"I know. I know. 'I'm too pretty by far,' as you once said."

"She's always been jealous of pretty girls, now she's jealous of any girl with legs. So you've got double daggers in your future if she spots you and recognizes you from before. So of course, once you get here, I don't know you."

"Well thanks again. I won't be expecting even a nod or a wink if I see you, unless I want a skillet thrown at me!"

"Take care, Jenny. And be careful around this Snooks guy, he looks like he could be real mean."

Snooks was the name Robert Brynes went by. It wasn't until I'd spent a week in Pahrump in a hotel room calling Wal-Mart Vision Centers non-stop that I'd learned his real name.

"How will I find him?"

"Booth 213. And the man does indeed have different colored eyes. He's selling some cleaning products, specialty oil products; tire stuff, and additives for RVs, and some new plumbing system. Everybody always has something new for plumbing."

"Well, after living in an RV, I can say that I appreciate anything that makes things flow smoothly in that arena."

He laughed. "Tell me about it, I've got three boys—I damned near have to wear a snake on my hip."

I laughed and wished him well then I hung up to ponder my project. It was too late to do anything with a printer today but I could get my RV cookbook ready for printing. Over a few glasses of wine I came up with a catchy title: *5 Ingredients, 5 Minute Prep, 5 Kisses.*

Inspired by Randy and his family, I found some clip art and fashioned a young woman sitting in an easy chair with her family surrounding her, her husband on his knees kissing her hand and three young boys (plus a girl to make it five), all were angling to kiss her cheeks.

I stayed up until two in the morning doctoring recipes, adding a few more, setting them up in sections, doing a table of contents and typing an index, and then formatting and paginating everything so it looked like a real cookbook. When I was done I had sixty-five pages of easy-to-prepare, five-ingredient recipes that I thought were scrumptious. I decided ten bucks would be the sale price and put that on the cover. Then I saved my file to a disc and to a flash drive, shut down the laptop, and dragged myself to bed. All was quiet, all was calm, but I knew that in a matter of just a few days, it would be anything but.

Lying in bed staring at the ceiling, I prayed I was doing the right thing by not telling Brick. Because right now, it would only take a word from me, and he'd be there. I wouldn't have to publish a book, buy things for a booth, and travel another couple hundred miles. And he'd have Jillie in his arms by nightfall.

Only the chance that I could be wrong in all this stopped me. I didn't think the man could stand another bad tip, wild goose chase, or false lead. Once I knew for sure that the girl with Robert Byrnes and his wife was really Jillie and not Anna, he could come in on a white charger and steal her away. I'd be fine with that. Hell, I'd be deliriously happy with that.

Chapter Twenty-six

Of course I didn't sleep a wink what with plotting and planning and worrying about getting the damned book ready. I knew Boise would have the best chance for a Kinko's-type printer, so after breakfast, I went online to check it out.

I found a FedEx shipping center that was combined with a Kinko's on North Milwaukee just a few block off Interstate 84. I called and found out I could email the file and pick up my spiral bound books in about four hours if I prepaid using my debit card over the phone. The bill was $368.

By the time I factored in the cost of the canopy and the fee I had to send with the vendor application, I would have over $500 invested in this scheme. Thank God I already had a collapsible table and chair. How did writers make any money doing this? They had to factor in gas and traveling expenses, which I was already committed to. But of course, that was not the goal here. I basically, just needed a cover. And selling a cookbook with recipes I had compiled myself was a good one. I'd have no trouble answering questions and mingling with both the crowd attending and the vendors behind the scenes. With any luck, I'd actually sell some books and recoup some of my costs.

I took a quick shower in the bathhouse, dressed for a

very warm day as it was already in the seventies, and packed everything up. I grabbed a handful of brochures at the office that I planned on handing out at The Rally. One had to support a fine, outstanding campground such as this. I made a mental note to go to RV Park Review and praise the hell out of this place.

As I was driving toward Boise, I got a call from the Rally coordinator saying they had accepted my vendor application and were looking forward to seeing the cookbook I had written. She said she also arranged to move the rally fee that I had already paid for attendance and for accommodations at the Deschutes County Fairgrounds, to the vendor fee and to the reduced-rate sites in the vendor area. I would have a refund coming unless I still chose to attend Peter Noonan's Concert and Vince Gill's concert. I didn't want to put her to any more trouble, so I said sure, I'd still attend. Yay! I was in.

I picked up the books, all five cases, and took a few minutes to marvel at my efforts. I had done a fantastic job and looking from an outsider's perspective, I thought it was easily worth ten bucks. I ended up selling two of them before I made it to the parking lot—one to the printer's assistant and one to the store manager—wow, only 98 to go.

At Wal-Mart I found a canopy called First-Up which promised an easy setup, and bought a package of poster board and some neon markers. Then I went to a bank and got cash to make change. I was in business! And pretty excited about my new endeavor if truth be known.

Leaving Boise, I decided to drive all the way to Redmond. It was only about 250 miles more. And as a vendor I could set up now, find my booth number, get a site for my RV and save myself the money I would spend on a campground tonight. Halfway there I went through the town of Burns and remembered exactly why I was here in the first place. Panic began to take over, I was afraid now that I was so close to the man Brick had sworn to kill. I had my hand on the phone to call Brick, ready to tell all, when the phone rang in my hand.

It was Gloria. Today was the first day we had agreed to do a daily check-in. I filled her in on my progress, told her about the book and had to agree to save one for her—97 to go. She told me about the tests they had to run on Daddy. He was having some problems with angina. I told her to give everyone my love and that I would try to find a way to see him as soon as I could. I was just about to disconnect when I heard Gloria gasp.

"What is it?" I almost ran into the other lane trying to navigate a turn while holding the phone. I punched the speaker button and dropped it into my lap.

"It's Jared!"

"There?" I hollered.

"No. On TV!"

"What's he done now?

"You aren't going to believe this, but he's escaped again. This time they were transporting him from the hospital back to Fairfax County Jail when he managed to get away. They found the officers handcuffed to the security cage on Route 7."

"Oh my God!"

"It's worse. Both officers were shot, one in the back, one in the hip."

"Sweet Jesus . . . how could he do that?"

"The officers say he was handcuffed in the back seat when they were rear ended. They both got out to check the damage and to see if anyone in the other car was hurt when two guys in the car that hit them attacked. Shots were fired. People driving by said they saw some men dragging the officers to the police car. When they turned around and came back, the attacker's car was missing."

"Oh he's really done it this time," I moaned.

"Yeah, but he's out now. And he's probably coming for you."

"He'll never find me here—the rig's been checked. I paid a man a hundred dollars at a Radio Shack in Kansas to go over the whole RV with that wand they have after the incident with

Jared and the twins. It did not pick up any transmitters. And I rolled my number over to a new cell phone just this morning. I've shut down my email program, and only you, Randy, and Brick even know about this rally."

"You just be careful. If I don't hear from you by ten every single morning, I'm calling Brick."

"That's what you're supposed to do, that's what we agreed you'd do."

"How long will it take that bastard to get all the way across the country if he's coming after you again?"

"Well I doubt that he'd fly, he has no I.D., no access to money, or at least not yet, he's a wanted man, and he's still pretty banged up I imagine."

"Yeah, the video they're showing on TV from the hospital monitor shows him limping from the wheelchair into the cruiser."

"So somehow he managed to arrange this accident and escape."

"Yeah, and now, according to the news, he has their guns. So if he can't fly how long will it take him to get to you once he figures out where you are?"

"Four, five days. Maybe three if he's with someone else and they never sleep. I don't really know."

"Well you need to plan on being out of there in three days then. Find the girl, do what you need to and get the hell away."

"That's the plan, Gloria. You take care. Give Dad a kiss for me, Mom too. I love you."

"Love you too."

I picked the phone up, took it off speaker and closed the case. Dear God, Jared had shot two officers! He could never return to his old life now. He truly had gone around the bend this time. It seemed the only thing that mattered to him now was getting to me. A man so obsessed with revenge that'd he give up everything he'd worked so hard for had to have spirochetes eating at his brain. If he found me this time, I knew he'd kill me.

Chapter Twenty-seven

It was four o'clock when I finally got to the fairgrounds. There was a volunteer to meet me who took my name, then another volunteer in a golf cart drove me around a mostly vacant parking lot that was gigantic, all the way over to another one on the backside that was already well-populated. It was mostly dirt, packed hard from years of use. It blended with the desert all around us and went on for what seemed like forever, until it abutted with the mountains. The Three Sisters Mountains off in the distance were a spectacular backdrop to the rows of RVs.

This was to be my village for the next few days. It was fairly bursting with excitement. People were setting up housekeeping, waving to each other as they passed, and loading all manner of things onto golf carts. It took ten minutes to get situated on the site, as the volunteer was very particular about everyone being on the lines spray-painted on the ground. This was clearly a structured event, everything would be precisely handled—it was more than apparent that the volunteers would see to that. I could see by their expressions how serious they were about their jobs. It was daunting. Begrudgingly, I made every maneuver he desired, indicated by his use of hand signals until he was satisfied I was where he wanted me. I put jack stands down and put the slide out and then I went outside to hook up to the multi-pronged utility pole that housed the electric connection. Setting up my own house was duck soup to me now.

Several people walked by and either nodded or waved, a few said "nice rig," and that's when I noticed that for once, mine was one of the newest and shiniest. I had forgotten this was the workingman's side. I got things together and set my little campsite up a few feet from the front door. I had a wonderful mesh mat in the basement that I put down to keep the dirt to a minimum inside the RV and two nice lounging chairs with a table between.

As this was a fairground and used for many things other than parking RVs, there were no water connections, sewer or otherwise, and no picnic table, grill, or fire ring. We were pretty much boondocking except for electricity. Mid-July anywhere out west without air conditioning would be grueling in this heat. And I was one of the ones who loved it hot, so I was happy when everything was working properly.

Suspecting that the bathhouse would be virtually empty this late, which it was, I took a shower, washed my hair and shaved before going back to my unit to dress in jean shorts and a t-shirt. A light snack of apple slices smeared with peanut butter and a tall glass of cranberry juice renewed me and I built up the courage to venture out into the world of the rally.

It was after the dinner hour for most, so those who didn't have children or chores to tend to gathered in clusters under colorful awnings. This was a different crowd. It had a reunion feel to it. Laughter rang through the air as people reconnected after months or years apart and with each new entry onto the lot, the men craned their necks to check out the new rig and to watch the set up process. Every camper was different and every rig had its idiosyncrasies. It was fascinating to see the unique ways people devised to handle everyday things. I watched one husband and wife spend many minutes and meticulous care getting their two dogs situated on tie outs as far from the rig as they could. I sensed they'd about had enough of their "children" for the day when I noted their license tag proclaimed them native to Maryland. Wow, they had to have been on the road for at least a week, no wonder they needed some space from their pets.

A woman named Nancy, on a walk with her own two mutts, came over and introduced herself and invited me to have some wine with her and her friends at her RV. Normally, I might have declined and opted to just be alone, but that was not why I was here. I needed to mingle, I need to interact—I needed to find Jillian. And since Gloria's phone call this morning, I realized I didn't have time for the luxury of anonymity.

I was welcomed into the little group of eight, introduced to Mary, Pat, Carl, Sharon, Jeff, Donetta, and Jobey, Nancy's husband. All very nice people who were pretty much on their way to being toasted, well except for Carl. He was spiking himself up on coffee, as he proclaimed when I was introduced, that he was one of the volunteer security guards, and tonight at midnight he would begin his first shift.

I figured that gave me an in, so I innocently asked, "What's going on at night?"

"Well, nothin' we hope. But a lot of people have their stuff set out already so the agreement is, we'll make sure you get to sell it. Don't rightly know that there's a whole lot of thievin' goin' on at these here kinda things, but I'll tell you one thing," and he leaned closer to me with his foul coffee and cigarette breathe and announced in an overly gregarious manner, "it's sure not gonna happen on my shift!"

I smiled and tried to inch my face away. "Good. Very good."

"You selling or toutin' sumpin'?"

I smiled, all bright and proud, not at all ashamed to peg myself as a novice for all the good it would do me. "Yes! I am. I have a cookbook that I wrote. It just came out and this rally will be its first try out."

All the women stopped talking and eyes agog, turned as

one to face me.

"A cookbook?" You'd think I'd said a twenty-carat diamond.

"You're a writer?" The way Pat beamed made me feel like a celebrity.

"You don't say?" Mild interest on the part of Donetta. "I don't cook anymore, you just don't have to with all the prepared foods out there." Her tunic top fought to cover her rounded body and if she dared to stand upright, it revealed a rather stretched out floral tattoo on her torso. What was once a rose stem was now more like a vine up her side. I could see how refined foods had insinuated themselves into her diet, and possibly Carl's too, as I thought she was paired with him. Why couldn't people stay beside their mates at these things, at least until I could figure out who went with whom?

And Nancy, bless her heart, "I want one. Let me go git ma money." She turned to leave then turned back with a grin, "I do git a discount now, being your neighbor and all?"

I smiled back, "Of course."

I went back to my unit to get her a book and she counted out eight ones. I thought a twenty percent discount appropriate among fellow vendors—96 to go. I drank the wine that was handed to me and recognized it as Charles Shaw, commonly known in RVing circles as Two-buck Chuck, even after it went to three dollars a few years back. I sipped it slowly as it sometimes left me with a tannin headache, while the women passed my cookbook around and oohed and aahed over it. They all had to have their own copy. Yes, even Donetta of refined foods, which I now, despite telling myself not to, associated with "doughn-etta." I traipsed back to the Dolphin and dug in the cardboard box for three more books. All of which now had to be equally discounted of course—93 to go.

After a few more minutes of idle conversation, I made my apologies, saying how tired I was from the drive, and made my way back to my RV. It was too soon to show my hand and ask any pertinent questions. I had a feeling a leisurely walk around the fairground tomorrow, after I had set up my wares and made myself one of the group, might net me more.

I drank a whole bottle of water, as everything seemed so dry here, and then I grabbed my book and a few Reese's Peanut Butter Cups before locking up and heading back to the bedroom.

The sheets felt cool and soft against my skin and I don't think I even finished one page before I was out, the heady taste of chocolate and sweet peanut butter melting against the roof of my mouth. I was tired and just the thought of what the following days would mean drained me of energy despite the sugar rush.

Chapter Twenty-eight

I woke to the sounds of people stirring in their campsites all around me. I opened my eyes and stared at the skylight for a few minutes trying to orient myself. Then before I could forget, I called my sister to check in, and as she belabored the fact that Jared was still "on the loose," I munched on the two remaining peanut butter cups I had unwrapped and left on the nightstand last night. Couldn't waste them could I, I asked myself as I popped one in my mouth and moaned.

"You sound like you're having sex," Gloria said with apparent disgust in her voice. Gloria had always been a grade A prude.

"Chocolate," I managed to mumble around the softening morsel.

"Ah, same thing. Only not quite so messy."

"You need a new partner. I never get the two confused."

"Are you having sex with that cop?"

"Uh, not at the moment, as I believe he's three or four states over. But if he was here . . .well, let's just say, there's not enough chocolate in the world."

"Geez, Deb—she never could get the name change imbedded in her brain—can't you get out of one relationship, one truly bad relationship, before starting another?"

"This is different."

"How?"

"He's not possessive." I thought about that for a moment. Yeah, yeah he was. "Well not as possessive." But he was, in his own way. "Well, in a good way."

"Debbie . . ."

"I know what I'm doing."

"You said that last time."

"I was too young to know what was going on. Believe me, I am not naïve anymore."

"What do you really know about this guy?"

"He treats me wonderfully. Hey! That's it! That's the difference."

I sat up as if I'd just had a eureka moment. "He cares about me. Me. You know, he isn't into sex at all unless it's to please me." The revelation had me kneeling on the bed smiling.

"I feel as if his pleasure is insignificant in the exchange. I really do feel as if I come first with him, and I didn't intend for that to be a pun."

"They're all like that at first. Then it's 'hey how 'bout a beer while I watch the game, and I wouldn't mind a . . .' as their hand circles their crotch."

"Boy you're a cynic. I'm the one who should be down on men, look what's happened to me."

"But it was only the one relationship."

"Have you had a bad relationship, Gloria?" I suddenly realized that lately all our conversations had been about me. "I know your marriage kind of petered out after awhile as you were both too career-minded to spend much time together, but I thought you were fine with Larry."

"Oh, he's okay," she said in a wistful voice. "You just seem to be having a lot more fun these days."

"Maybe it's because I wake up eating chocolate."

"I'll have to give that a try. Gotta run. Don't forget I want a cookbook."

"Gotcha." I popped the other chocolate into my mouth and smiled.

The phone rang and I saw it was Brick. Good news or bad, I debated as I flipped the cover up.

"Good morning Beautiful, how's my girl?"

Nervous, edgy, scared, and probably only a football field's length from your sister, I thought, but instead came up with "Great. Just great. How 'bout you?"

"Couldn't be better. Just wrapped up a case I was the expert witness on and in about an hour I'll be on a plane heading back west."

"Do you get paid for being an expert witness?"

"Yes and no. I have to charge a fee otherwise there'd be no end to it. Unless it's one of our own cases, it's on my own time, but I usually donate the fee to one of the reward programs for missing kids. Or to the injured family if there's no conflict, if it's that kind of case. Why do you ask?"

"Just wondering, you always seem to have money. Not like most cops."

"Well, I *am* single, with no mortgage or rent, my travel expenses are paid for by the jurisdiction I'm working for, and I don't seem to have time for an expensive hobby. Hell, I can't even find time for you—pleasuring you being my most favorite hobby by far."

I felt the blush creep up the side of my face. "So where are you flying back to?"

"North Dakota. I left my rig close to the Canadian border. We extradited a child rapist they picked up forging checks. I had to accompany the agent making the arrest and had to leave it at a ranger station. After that I have to speak at a high school on the pros and cons of oral sex."

"Hmmm . . . I was pretty sure you were for it."

"For adults."

"Were you for it when you were in high school?"

143

"Mmmm . . . plead the fifth. *However*, things have changed greatly since I was in high school."

"Give me a for instance."

"Okay. Say you've got a girlfriend, she's fourteen and you're sixteen. She offers to give you head and you accept. She initiates everything. Having sex with her this way is a felony in most states, particularly if the boy is over 16. At 14 the girl is not able to consent to this even though it was her idea and she carried it out without any help from him. It is considered an act of rape even with it being voluntary on her part. So, a week later, she sees him flirting with another girl, and he gets charged with rape because she's angry. His life is ruined even though he was innocent of any kind of abuse or coercion in the act."

"Wow."

"Yeah. My job is to intervene before an innocent boy gets charged with a crime, is taken out of school, sent to jail and listed on a state sex offender list. So, while yes, I could have let Janine suck me off on the back seat of my dad's Lincoln, I would not have had to deal with any of that."

"Did you?"

"Many times. That sucking the chrome off the trailer hitch thing became a real popular saying with the guys she went out with."

"Wouldn't think you'd want someone sucking quite that hard," I said.

"There is a knack to it, too hard doesn't get the job done, that's for sure. Interestingly enough, we're now finding out that some moms are teaching their daughters that oral sex is the way to get the boy they want, and a few are even schooling their girls in how to perform it."

"They're not all that wrong about it being the way to get the boy."

"No, they're certainly not wrong about that. But that's not the way it's supposed to be."

"Love shouldn't be about sex?" I couldn't keep the edge

of droll out of my tone.

"No, at least not one-way sex."

"Am I the only one getting horny here?" I asked, picturing myself on my knees in front of him, pleasuring him as *Janine* had.

"Are you kidding, I've had to face the wall since I heard your sexy voice."

"So we may be able to rendezvous someplace after this rally?"

"You betcha. I've finagled a few weeks off. I thought we might park one of the RVs and tour the Napa Valley. How does that sound to you?"

It sounded wonderful, but if things went according to plan he'd likely be spending those weeks off reuniting his sister with his family. But I knew if I didn't voice my pleasure he'd wonder why. "Mmmm wine. I love wine."

"I know you do. And so do I. We'll get something sparkling and pink that I can drink from your navel . . . and from that sweet little pink honey pot."

I blushed full bore then. "Mmmm . . . sounds, well sounds kinda cold actually. Brrr."

"Oh baby, I'm gonna heat you up with little nips and kisses, make you so hot that you'll beg me to dribble some chilled . . . oops, gotta go! They're calling my flight, gotta clear my gun. Remind me where I left off."

"You'll call me when you're back on the road?"

"I'll probably call you tonight. Have fun at the rally!"

"Thanks. Oh by the way, did you hear about Jared?"

But he was gone. I could picture him handsome as all get out, the ultimate bad boy in a business suit, drawing the eye of every available woman as his long legs strode through the airport on the way to his gate. I knew he traveled with his laptop, I hadn't known he traveled with his gun. That must make for some fun times at security checkpoints, I thought as I closed my phone.

I looked around for another piece of chocolate and having found none, got out of bed and stretched. I did a few Eka Pada and Parivratta Janu stretches, to wake up my thighs, calves and ribcage, ending with a Purvottanasana reclining pose to stretch out my back. I was ready to face the day, whatever it might bring.

I told myself not to expect too much today, that today was just about wandering around, getting the feel for the place, and doing some recon. That it wasn't likely I'd run into Robert Byrnes, his wife or Jillie as there were so many vendors here, over three hundred if the publicity could be believed. But I had to be ready in case I did.

I pulled on a pair of jeans and a t-shirt, ran a brush through my hair and used a clip to secure it to the back of my head. Today was a workday; I would set up my little booth in the building being utilized for the vendors. I would set everything out except for the actual books, which I would take over tomorrow when The Rally officially opened to the public.

Realizing that chocolate might not sustain me for long, I tucked a Kashi bar into my back pocket and grabbed a bottle of water.

There was hardly anyone around when I left the RV to head over to the main buildings. They offered breakfast during the rally, but today, everyone was still fending for themselves, but I could smell the kitchens preparing something for tomorrow, something with grilled onions and peppers, reminiscent of Mexican fajitas. My mouth watered and I made plans for a more substantial lunch.

It was quite a walk, but I found my assigned spot easily enough and then asked to borrow a handtruck I saw leaning against the wall. My neighbor was a husband and wife team demonstrating products for a company called MCD Innovations; they had come all the way from Texas to be here. They had a double-sized booth so they could display all the types of shades and window coverings they offered as well as these really cool slide on wheel covers I coveted. We immediately hit it off and

I jauntily pushed the handtruck through the aisles and down the pavement to the parking lot and from there to my RV where I loaded my table and chair, and the canopy, and the sign I had made. Things were so spread out that I knew I'd be getting a fair amount of exercise just walking back and forth.

On the way back I looked at all the other displays and realized this was all pretty professionally done. Customized booths, tables with special coverings and drapes, racks and stands with display cases. My card table and sign were going to look pretty lame.

I was mentally going through my linens deciding if I had anything I could piece together for a table drape when I practically walked into a man coming around the corner. We actually did collide. I grabbed my table to keep it from sliding off the dolly and he grabbed me to keep me from falling. I gasped looked up into his face and froze. The man holding me by the shoulders and looking down into my face was Randy and as soon as I focused on his eyes, I knew this was no chance encounter. With his pursed lips and a hardly discernible shake of his head he warned me not to acknowledge him—with eyes shifting to the right, he alerted me to why. Booth 213 was right in front of me and a tall man with a swarthy tan and two different colored eyes looked over at us.

"You okay?" Randy asked, solicitous and apologetic as he clearly accepted our collision as his fault.

"Yes, yes, I'm fine."

"Well I'm sorry, I should have been looking where I was going." Clearly he had seen me coming and waylaid me on purpose. He had wanted me to see who was in the booth behind him.

"No harm done."

"Here, let me help you with that."

"Oh I can manage." But I didn't protest too much as I knew he was trying to get me away so he could talk to me.

"I can easily carry that table with one hand and save you

all that jostling. Least I can do."

Before I could say yay or nay, he hoisted the table under his arm and put his arms out as if asking me to lead the way.

When we were out of both ear and eye shot, I said with awe, "That's him."

"Yup, that's him."

"Have you seen her today?"

"No, just saw him this morning in the bathhouse. Kinda followed him back here. He's only about five booths down from me. His company's pretty big time, they've got one of the largest displays. He and another guy are setting it up."

"Great. Once I get my stuff set up, I'll mosey on back and check it out."

"Be careful . . ."

"Oh I will be. Charlotte and the kids here?"

"They're helping to set up the children's tent. Charlotte's going to be a storyteller. The kids are real excited about that as it's the first time she's been involved since the accident."

"Well that's great news."

"Yeah."

"So what's the plan here?"

"No plan, at least not yet. I have to make sure this guy's daughter is Jillie before I can do anything. So today I set up, tomorrow I sell cookbooks, and in between times, I check things out."

"Then what? What if it *is* her?"

"Then I call in the cavalry."

"Okay, stick to the plan. Don't go all maverick on me."

"Maverick?" I said as I smiled up at him. We had arrived at my booth now and he was swinging the table out and setting it up.

"Yeah. A horse that runs wild and gets herself in trouble."

"Oh. Now that you mention it, I do have that tendency."

"Curb it. You be careful." He shook his finger at me and stalked off.

In a matter of minutes, Jim and I had the canopy up. I hurriedly slapped my sign up and returned the handcart to my neighbors. I worked my way over to the section close to where Randy and I had collided. Then I whipped my Kashi bar out and munched on it as I took in all the other displays. Trying to look interested in everything, I paid attention to each booth, asking questions and showing interest while trying not to deter anyone from their job. It took about twenty minutes until I finally made my way to Booth 213. I casually scanned all the brochures and took in the products on display. I was mindful not to react to either the sound or appearance of Robert Byrnes when he deigned to notice and acknowledge me. But he didn't.

I could feel him watching me, from the corner of my eye I had seen him dismiss me as an innocent gawker. Well I couldn't have that. I would have to initiate some contact. Fortunately I was well versed in gasoline additives, which seemed to be the bulk of the products at the center table. "Does this work as well as Mileage Booster?" I asked as I pointed to the plastic gallon jug.

He looked up and walked over. I looked up and met his eyes. *Don't stare* I told myself, don't even react. You're asking about gas additives for God's sake, nothing else.

"Well actually it's better than Mileage Booster, it lasts longer because it doesn't break down in the engine as fast. So a gallon of this could easily last a year. And most manufacturers approve it for their gas engines. What kind of rig do you have and how many miles a year do you drive?"

"I've got a class A, and right now I'm at ten thousand for the year."

"Then you could save yourself some money in the long run by using this every time you fill-up."

"How much is it?"

"Sixty-eight dollars. For vendors, I can make it fifty."

"Sold. I've wanted to try something like this for a long time. I'll bring you some cash later today or tomorrow."

"That would be great." I already knew from talking to other vendors that cash was highly preferred over charge cards as they had to pay a percentage to the credit card companies.

I checked out the table of slide-out lubes, rubber seal conditioners, black streak removers, and awning cleaners. Then intrigued by a product called SunBlock for tires, I picked it up. He came back to give me another spiel. It seemed like a lot of work as you had to pre-treat with tire prep for the best results, but the claim that it lasted four to five years was major. He gave me a handout and I promised to read it and decide. I had tire covers but they were a real pain to put on. I could see how this one product could keep you busy singing praises at a rally like this if it really worked.

He turned to get back to the box he was unloading from and I crammed the Kashi bar I had been squeezing in my fist, into my mouth, ripping off a huge chunk. Not very ladylike, but it kept me from gasping for air. Sweat was pooling under my armpits, between my breasts and beading on my back. I could feel my hairline dampening despite the cooling breeze blowing from one end of the huge building to the other.

I moved to the next booth, continuing my foray until I felt I was far enough away that I could stop pretending to admire the displays and change course. It was time to walk around the vendor campsites to see if I could figure out which one Jillie could be in.

I picked up the pace and made an abrupt halt at a novelty booth selling potholders, dish towels, bath towels and linens. Some were made of the popular micro fiber so prevalent at fairs such as these and used so efficiently to clean RVs inside and out. At the front of the table was a pile of embroidered linens, the type used to line a breadbasket or grace a sommelier's arm. I was drawn to the lovely colors and patterns as well as the practical aspects. I fingered through the piles and found a combination of colors that I liked and asked how much six of them would be. We agreed on a price and I pulled some cash from my front pocket. These would be perfect, I thought as I carried my newfound treasures back to the RV campground.

Hugging the soft linens to my chest I made my way back to my RV, taking the long way around and checking out each site, its occupants if they were out and about, and incidentally starting off a chorus of barking as I passed by the ones being "protected" in the owner's absence. No little girl, no little boys either.

Finally back at my Dolphin I laid out the panels I had bought with a specific purpose in mind and I set to work sewing. I had some potholders and an apron with embroidered foodstuffs on it, so I attached them in the appropriate places, fanning the apron out in the middle. By the time I was done I had a nice drape that would draw the eye—a slice of pizza here, a fudge sundae there, chocolate cake and a cheeseburger off to the side—it was like a quilt made of dish towels with a menu theme. It was perfect for showcasing my cookbook. Then I selected two recipes from the book and made samples for tasting. The mini pizzas made using portabella mushrooms as the crust, jarred marinara as the sauce, and strips torn from string cheese and pepperoni pieces as the toppings. Four ingredients, but usually I skipped the pepperoni and made it with three. I made some both ways in case there were vegetarians in the crowd. Then I made my recipe for heart healthy brownies: a box of dark chocolate brownie mix, a 15 oz. can of black beans drained and a cup of water. Pureeing the bean mixture would be a problem for most RVers, as most didn't travel with food processors. But many had blenders to make cocktails in and that worked just as well. I just stuck my immersion blender right in the can. Anyway, they smelled delicious while they were cooking and with only two ingredients, as they never counted water or salt and pepper in these types of cookbooks, they were sure to be a hit. I made two batches and cut the squares bite-sized to feed as many rally goers as possible.

I was about as ready as I could be for opening day, though

technically most vendors were already open for the early bird days. I opted to wait, as I wanted everything perfect.

After lunch I took the table covering over and set up the display, moving the sign this way and that to see what drew the eye better from six to eight feet away.

As I was scoping it out and adjusting it against the table skirt I had made, a few people came by who were interested in buying the cookbook. I offered to go get a few and came back with a case of books, my bank bag, and a tray of the brownies. What the heck, if there were customers I might as well start now.

I was soon out of books and brownies and had to go back for more. I exchanged my sandals for sneakers as I was getting a pretty good workout going back and forth and my feet were beginning to get tender and my calves were burning. I had no sooner set up a new stack of books and set out the brownies when Robert Byrnes walked up to the table. I could see there was someone behind him in a dress, but I couldn't see who it was since he was a pretty big man. My heart went into a raging staccato at the thought that it might be Jillie.

He smiled and said, "I hear you have some might tasty brownies, everyone's talkin' about them . . . and your cookbook. You mind if my daughter and I sample one?"

I looked up, my eyes wide, and made myself smile back. *Steady girl, calm down. Just give them each a brownie and talk about the book.* "Of course not, please help yourself."

As I lifted the tray in offering, a young girl came from around her father's side. I had to swallow my gasp and stop my rough inhale in mid-progress. Jillie. There was no doubt about it. None whatsoever. She was a female Brick in miniature— her coloring was fair, she had no tan, and her hair was brown tinted with auburn where his was almost black. But she had his vivid eyes, his fine nose, his full lips, his high cheekbones, his sculpted eyebrows. She even had his little dimple in the center of her chin.

I forced myself to look away and focus on Robert's hand

on the tray as he selected two brownies.

He turned and placed one in the girl's hand before lifting his to his mouth. "Mmm . . . not bad. I like mine with nuts, but this is pretty good. Only two ingredients like the sign says, and heart healthy?"

"Yup. Well, plus a little water. The recipe's in the book." I took a cookbook, placed it in front of them and turned the pages as I told them about each recipe. As I was finishing up my spiel, Robert turned to his daughter and said, "So what'dya think? You think your ma would like this cookbook?"

The girl nodded eagerly and Robert dug in his pocket and came out with a wad of cash.

"Sign says ten dollars, that right?"

"Well, as one vendor to another, I'm pleased to offer a discount. Make it eight."

Robert peeled off eight ones and handed them to the girl, who handed them to me.

"It's her ma's birthday tomorrow. This'll make a fine gift from her Annie."

I took the money from the girl and handed her a book, saying thank you. The girl smiled and took it from me and not wanting to let her go, I grabbed her fingers for just a second. Covering the impulsive act, I moved them over to the tray. "Here, have another brownie. Once you see what's in them you'll realize they're actually good for you!"

"Thank you, thank you very much," she said very politely and helped herself to another. I lifted the tray to Robert. "You too."

He also took another brownie. Then he wrapped his big arm around her small shoulders and led her away.

I stood staring after them. Then made myself eat a brownie so I wouldn't look so focused on the two of them getting further away.

Dear God. I put my head down and pinched the bridge of my nose. I need to think. I needed to breathe. I needed wine in large quantities. But more than anything, right now I needed Brick. The seriousness of what was happening was sinking in now. This was real . . . this was about a little girl's life. This was about a mother's life . . . Brick's mother's life. And her father's. And this was also about Brick's life. I was holding their happiness, their future, in my hand. It was suddenly too much responsibility; too much to be in charge of. I became aware of a voice slightly above and behind me. I was startled from the suddenness of it. It was Jim, the vendor next to me.

"You're going to have to bake a few more batches tonight. At the rate you're selling those books, you're going to be out of them tomorrow. How many did you say you brought?"

"A hundred."

"You're definitely going to run out."

I looked up at him, I couldn't generate a smile, even though I thought that would be the mostly likely expression someone would have after hearing what he'd just said. But it just wouldn't come. "Maybe. But that's a good thing, right?"

"Sure. You sell out then you can close down and head on out or just enjoy the rally as a spectator. It's a good problem to have. Can you get more?"

I thought about that. Yes, yes I could. I could certainly get more. I shrugged my shoulders. "Yeah, I suppose."

"Might be worth it to try."

"We'll see how tomorrow goes, I can always go into town and have more printed if there's a Kinko's around."

"Might be one in Bend."

Bend was a neighboring city, south of Redmond; it was a bit more cosmopolitan and had lots of boutiques and charming little restaurants. It was possible they had a printer that could handle a short run print job. But that really wasn't where my mind was. My mind was on that little girl, walking with the man she thought of as her dad, with a gift in her hand for the woman she thought of as her mom—I knew differently.

Chapter Twenty-nine

At four o'clock things wound down as people wanted to get ready for the cocktail hour before dinnertime. It was still the evening before the official start of The Rally, but things were happening. People were making plans to hook up and there was much revelry. I was glad to gather up my things and shuffle home. I was in some kind of funk, I thought it might be from the adrenaline ebbing and flowing like waves crashing on the shore.

A brisk shower at the bathhouse invigorated me and I walked back with a determined bounce to my step. I tried to call Brick, but it went right to voicemail. He must still be traveling, I thought. Then I called Gloria, and her phone, while it rang and rang, no one answered. On the ninth ring the machine finally answered with a curt, "Leave a message."

I left one equally as curt. "Found her. She's here. Excited and scared. I'll call you in the morning."

I put on some capris and a soft summer sweater to match, slid my feet into thong-type sandals and made my way to the building designated as the dining hall for tonight. I was in my own little world thinking about logistics and what I could do next when up ahead I made out a man and a girl walking two huge dogs, golden retrievers if I wasn't mistaken. I squinted and stared harder. It was Robert Brynes and Annie. They had both changed their clothes, she was now in shorts with a ruffled top, he was in black jeans with a Hawaiian shirt. At first, I was going to pretend I hadn't seen them, detour through someone's lot and join the road on the other side, but a sudden boldness drew me up. I waved as they drew nearer and when they were only a few feet away, I played on every dog lover's sense of pride, and knelt and cooed over the dogs. Big tongues lapped at my hands and tried for my face while huge plumed tails whipped against my thighs nearly knocking me off my feet.

Annie came and bent beside me. "They like you, you must taste like brownies."

"I hope not. I took a nice long shower as I was sure I was gaining a pound with each whiff."

"Not hardly," Robert Brynes said with a chuckle, and just the fact that he had noticed me in that way sent a chill through my spine. I hoped and prayed that he had found nothing more than a daughter to replace the one he'd lost in Annie. I forced myself to look up and smile. "I have some dog treats I made from recipes in the book, would you mind if I gave them some?"

He smiled down at me and said, "I'm sure David and Goliath would love to have them."

I stood up and made to leave, "My RV's right there," I said pointing. "The Dolphin, I'll be right back.

He said, "Annie'll go with you, I'll finish walking them as we have to get back to help with dinner."

"Great." And it really was. I'd have Annie to myself for a few minutes. But as soon as Annie and I started walking back to the RV, I panicked. If I showed my hand, she could do any matter of things, including tipping her parents off. What if she was so totally assimilated that she was only loyal to them now. I knew all about the Stockholm Syndrome and the emotional attachments that led to. The Brynes were her parents now, had been for four years—just about all of her recallable life. I couldn't force her to betray that trust as long as they were anywhere around. I opted for safe. Questions anyone would ask in a similar situation.

"So, you have any brothers or sisters?"

"No. I had a brother once, but he died."

"Oh, I'm so sorry." But a door had been opened and as if a cool draft had wafted over me, I had a suspicion hit me in the face.

"What was his name?"

"Brick, but I called him Baboo."

I feigned tripping though nothing was in my way, just to cover up my gasp and the reaction my hands had at her mentioning Brick's name. I was clutching my chest as if trying to keep my heart from jumping out of my chest.'

"You okay?" she asked, very concerned and leaning into me.

I recovered enough to mumble something about these stupid sandals and how I needed to lift my feet instead of drag them.

"Yeah, my mom tells me that all the time."

It was a good time to stay with that train of thought. If I asked any more questions about Brick, like how he had died, I knew I would lose my composure and make her suspicious of me.

"Yeah, my mom told me that, too. But as you can see, it never sunk in." We were at my RV now, so I took my key from my pocket and unlocked the door. "You want to come in for a minute?"

She took a quick look up the street and saw her dad with the dogs in the field. He was in turn watching her. "No, I'd better not. Dad's waiting."

"Okay, I'll be right back." I ran inside and found the treats I had made a few weeks ago for some other camper's dogs, mostly to shut them up whenever I walked by and they were out. I'd saved some in Ziploc baggies and took two baggies out of the cabinet so each dog could have its own bag. Making friends with these dogs seemed a smart thing to do at this point.

Not wanting to keep Annie waiting, and in turn annoying her dad, I rushed out the door and gave her the bags. Taking the initiative and saying goodbye first seemed prudent. I didn't want to appear clingy, curious, or anxious to keep her near, yet I really didn't want to let her go. There was just so much to lose by calling attention to myself and making them wonder about me.

But Annie just seemed genuinely happy to get the treats for her dogs and unfailingly polite when I said I had to be going, that I was meeting someone at the dining hall, which was so not true.

We waved good-bye and I even turned and waved good-bye to Robert before going back to lock the door again before heading back out.

The dining hall was packed and it was a boisterous crowd that was clamoring for free drinks and food. It was fun to watch so many happy people. Most had had a good day "in the stalls" as they called it, and were looking forward to the official opening of The Rally tomorrow. Tomorrow night Bobby Vinton would be wowing the crowd with his legendary songs, *Roses are Red*, *Mr. Lonely*, and *Blue Velvet* among others. And two nights later Peter Noone, better known as Herman of Herman's Hermits, would be reminding them all of the British Invasion that fairly consumed the entertainment world during the 60s and 70s.

I found that you couldn't stand in line for anything and not find a friend and as soon as they learned that I was the "Brownie Lady," I was practically given a throne. Most of the vendors were of the opinion that I would sell out by tomorrow, asking many questions about the process of coming up with the book so presumably they could try their hand at it too. Some asked why I hadn't had more faith and brought five hundred books to the rally. By the end of the evening I was giddy from the free-flowing wine and a little drunk on the overwhelming camaraderie.

I fended off a few chummy fellas who were solo on this trip and managed to side step one rather amorous Lothario who at eighty thought he was God's gift. He must have told me ten times about his secret stash of Viagra, in hopes I'd take him up on allowing him to show me how well it worked. As I was leaving so was Randy. I saw Charlotte in her wheelchair ahead of him and the boys surrounding her to clear the way so I thought it was safe to sidle up and whisper. "Found her."

He stilled momentarily and then turned to see who it was who was whispering so close to his ear. As soon as he saw me his eyes lit and he smiled. I watched as the message registered. His eyes widened and he blinked his eyes in shock. "Really? You did?"

Just then I saw Charlotte turn and look back at us. I pushed against his shoulder, gave him a scathing look and pointed at my toe. His baffled look was almost comical until he heard me say sotto voce, "Charlotte's looking back. Pretend you stepped on my foot."

Instantly his hands went up in a defensive gesture and he began to apologize profusely. "I'll call you later if I can," he mumbled and hurried to catch up with his family.

Charlotte was still looking back so I limped for a few feet before hobbling over to a seat. When they were out of sight I got up and made my way to the door. My 80-year old gentleman, who was no gentleman at all, was waiting for me.

"Kin I walk ya home, Sweetie? Girl on her own shouldn't oughta be on her own afta dark."

Reading his name off his name tag, I said, "Pardon my bluntness, Mr. Gene Weinger, but I think this 'girl' on her own after dark is far safer with hoodlums and thieves, so I think I'll be making the trek back to my RV on my own, but thank you for the offer."

He pouted and looked genuinely surprised that I had refused his offer, and mumbling something about me not knowin' what I was missin', he sauntered off to find a willing participant for his new lease on life. I wondered idly if he'd discovered this miracle drug before or after his wife had died. If it was before, I had no doubt it had hastened her path to the grave.

"Happy Hunting," I called back half-heartedly over my shoulder. I took my time walking back to the RV hoping to see where the Brynes lived, regretting I hadn't found a way to follow them home earlier.

When I got home, there was a tiny note tucked into the doorframe. Hand painted, the cover of the tiny card had a picture of David and Goliath tugging on a baggie filled with treats. It was adorable and very well done. I opened the card to read,

Thank you for the lovely treats,
I assure you they didn't last long.
I've already written down the ingredients from the book
so I can make more.
Your lovely cookbook is wrapped as a gift for Momma now.
Thank you ever so much,
Annie

I smiled and touched the card to my chest. What a sweet kid. I went inside to find my phone to see if Brick had called. He hadn't. I tried his number again, and again it went right to voicemail. I forgot when he said he'd be back in North Dakota. He must still be enroute I thought as I dressed for bed. I wondered if I should leave a message or try to track down his boss, Joe Rydell. I brushed my teeth and washed my face then took my book to bed to read. I doubt I finished the first paragraph before I dropped it to the floor and slid down with the pillow still propped at my back. It had been a long day and I was bushed. Surely I would get in touch with Brick tomorrow.

Chapter Thirty

My first thought upon waking, was damn, I forgot to set the alarm, the second was that I was supposed to be set up and ready in fifteen minutes. Shit.

I ran around getting things together: me, the food samples, my bank bag, some fruit, bottled water and an energy bar for lunch, and then I dashed over to the craft and vendor building. I'd taken a scant few minutes to wash my face, brush my teeth, gargle, secure my hair in a ponytail, swipe some blusher over my cheeks and smear some lip gloss on. Coffee and a breakfast biscuit from one of the food vendors would have to do this morning as I'd missed the wonderful breakfast buffet everyone had been raving about last night.

I quickly set up my area and then practically knelt at Jim and Peggy's feet when they brought me some coffee and a Danish. I'd been afraid I'd eat my pineapple angel food cake samples for breakfast. It would have taken a dozen one-inch squares to satisfy like this cinnamon apple confection. Peg said she brought it from the dining hall but was too full to eat it. I doubly missed having woken too late to make breakfast. This was scrumptious. I had to put it aside for my first customer who bought three of the cookbooks for gifts.

After that, I don't remember much of anything except taking praise for my samples, signing cookbooks, and smiling as people handed over wads of cash. The remaining books disappeared in less than three hours. I hadn't even had the foresight to save one for my sister before I realized I had sold the last one. I looked over at Peggy and Jim and smiled with chagrin, "What now?" I asked. They were between customers and came over to smile down at me.

"I guess you'd better go get some more. You got a winner there!"

I stood, gathered my tote bag and the sign. "Okay, I'd better see about doing that. Thanks for all your help." As an afterthought I pulled a marker from my bag, wrote SOLD OUT! GOING FOR MORE! on the sign and left it in the center of the table on top of the colorful tablecloth I'd made with pictures of snack foods all over it. Gripping the bag that held the bank bag and the book I thought I might have time to read between customers, I waved to the vendors around me as I "walked off the job."

I knew I wasn't going to order any more books. But I couldn't take down the table with my display and just leave, or they'd know it too. For now, it served for all to know that I'd sold out and that I was off getting more books to sell. Most would think that a good idea with The Rally just beginning. What I *was* going to do was find out where the heck Brick was. I hadn't made my ten o'clock call to my sister, so with any luck she'd managed to track him down by now.

Arriving back at my RV and dumping my stuff on the sofa, I reached for the phone and saw I'd missed two calls. Both were from Gloria. I tried to reach both her and Brick but couldn't get either. Practically screaming my rage and frustration, I paced, hoping to hear back from them within the next few minutes.

After an hour I couldn't stand the waiting anymore. I knew I had to continue the charade just so I could keep an eye on Jillie. It would not do for her to disappear again. Brick would kill me. I grabbed the Rally schedule and read all the events going on today. There were several seminars I would have liked to go to, but as agitated as I was I knew I couldn't sit for any length of time even though some of them sound really good. *Honey Let's Clean the RV— Have RV . . . Will Travel . . . Where to?— The Pros and Cons of RV Extended Warranties— RV Solarshades: Be Quick, Be Cool, Be Private—Water Pressure in the RV— Water Filtration, Purification & Conditioning— Controlling Odors in Holding Tanks & Water Heaters—RV Lubrication . . .* Whoa! RV Lubrication . . . I remembered seeing the sign on the display at Robert Byrne's stall. I remembered it listed the dates and times of his seminar. At three o'clock he'd be teaching. So who would be minding the booth with his partner, it was far too busy a booth to manage with only one person.

I decided to take a walk over and find out, maybe it was Jillie. I grabbed a PB & J sandwich, and a Pepsi, a rarity for me, but every once in a while I just felt like a soda. I also had to have a little bag of Frito's to go with it. I was in a rare mood; it seemed I needed sugar, carbs, and caffeine. I was pumped. Primed for action. I'd already had lunch earlier but for some reason I was starved. It was like I was preparing for a fast, storing up calories for energy.

I ate while I forced myself to stroll instead of eating the ground up with long strides. I had to appear normal, relaxed, agenda-less. I approached the "lubrication" booth from the side and saw that a woman was manning it. I'd seen her working alongside Robert on that first day when they were getting set up, she'd been in the back writing on boxes. I thought she might be his wife, but I wasn't sure. She spotted me, smiled hugely and waved me over. I swallowed, smiled back and made my way over to her. Whoever she was, she obviously knew who I was.

"I had a lovely present waiting for me this morning, your beautiful cookbook and homemade brownies Annie made for me! She can't wait for me to go to the store so I can get what she needs for David & Goliath's treats. That was so sweet of you!"

She had a pleasant Irish brogue, one that was born to the tongue and not easily discarded.

"Oh you're welcome. And Happy Birthday."

"Not much of one today, I'm afraid. Robert's doin' the seminars and Annie's gone to the Youth Group to watch the teens dance and have some pizza. I'm havin' to cover for him instead of being with her and her friends. Oh well, a fine birthday for me it will be if I get home and get a chance for a cuppa tea with no one about. Annie though, she might not last to have a bite of my cake tonight, got a bee sting ya know."

"Really? Is it bad?"

"No, never has been before. Just the Benadryl I gave her makes her sleepy sometimes. I worry at how strong those tiny pills are for her wee self."

"I'll go check on her if you like. I've nothing to do. I sold all the books."

"Yes, I heard. Glad I got mine in time. Sure if you don't mind. Take our golf cart, it's the green one by the front door. If she needs to go home, it'll be easy to get her there. Oh, I've got customers. Here's the key."

She handed me the key and I took it. "Thanks, I'll have a piece of pizza with her, see how she's doing." I'd said it in jest but the idea had its appeal. How could I possibly want pizza after having had an energy bar, an apple, a sandwich, Fritos, and a soda? Normally that much food would have had me on overload. Was the state of agitation I was in burning food like tinder in an inferno?

Gosh what a nice lady, I thought as I slid onto the seat of the cart and plugged in the key. It was hard to believe that she'd take someone's child. For the first time I wondered if this was all Robert's doing.

I wasn't sure where the youth were meeting, but one of the volunteers on the corner of the main intersection pointed me in the right direction.

Turning the corner I could see that the Fairgrounds had

filled up. The 132 acres that was the Deschutes County Fairground and Expo Center were packed with row after row of RVs. It was an impressive sight and now I knew why the volunteers were such sticklers for the tires being on the lines—4500 recreational vehicles in perfect diagonal rows was mind-boggling. Like a field of campers planted against the ruggedness of the terrain, it went on seemingly forever. In the VIP parking were the promotional RVs for Good Sam's Club, Coast to Coast, Trailer Life, Woodall's, Camping World, Dish Network, you name it; anything having to do with camping was represented here. It was quite a show. I passed the section where they had over a thousand RVs on display, all for sale and able to be made ready for the road in a few hours. As my eyes took it all in, I thought the beauty of the Cascades as the backdrop made it some kind of pop-art statement of the times. I wished that I had my camera. I'd have to remember to get it and come back. The vantage point where I was, where the volunteer tents were, had the best view as many people were walking up the hill to take pictures.

I realized I was blocking traffic so I moved on and took in the sights as even more RVs were lined up to get into the fairgrounds.

I finally got to the big tent and parked by the opening. I could hear loud music blaring from the back of it. I doubted that Annie could sleep through that. I slid off the seat, separated the fold of the tent and walked inside. I was met by one of the counselors and when I told her why I was there she smiled with relief and pointed to a table set off to the side. There in the middle of an otherwise empty table was a russet-colored head resting on crossed arms. Annie was asleep.

I explained that I had the Bryne's cart and that I would drive her home. She and one of the heftier boys helped me get her to the cart, and then I laid her head in my lap and slowly drove her down the hill and around the bend to the vendor RV sites. As I was entering the section I remembered that I didn't know where she lived. I shook her shoulder, Annie?"

"Mmmgh?"

"Annie, wake up."

"Unnnuuhhh."

"Jillie, I don't . . ." Uh oh, I had used her real name. Then an idea so preposterous it floored me leapt to the forefront of my mind. I hit the brake so suddenly she almost slid off the seat. I grabbed her by her belt and hauled her back up.

I sat running my hand through her hair. I could take her to *my* RV. I could tuck her inside, tear down, and head out with her before anyone knew what was up. Most of the vendors were expecting me to pull out to get more books. Annie wouldn't be missed until either Robert or his wife got back to their RV. I looked at my watch. I had maybe a two-hour lead. I stopped thinking. I put my foot down on the gas pedal and drove.

Chapter Thirty-one

It was probably the best time to be doing something nefarious at the vendor campground as just about everybody was at the stalls this time of day. It was getting close to wrap up time and this was the make hay part of the day as everyone was making their second pass, buying the things they didn't want to carry around all day.

I only saw one person and thankfully, she was to the left of me and wasn't able to see Annie, lying face down with her head in my lap. I stroked a strand of flaming red hair off my thigh and then waved with my hand to deflect her eyes from the seat. The woman was eighty if she was a day, and I prayed her eyesight was typical of a woman her age and that she couldn't see Annie slumped beside me. I idly wondered if this could be Viagra-man's wife and then chastised myself for going so far off what I should be focusing on.

I finally saw my Dolphin ahead and while I would have opted to park the cart on the opposite side, away from what I knew to be prying eyes, I wasn't sure how easy it was going to be getting Annie inside. I needed to get her in fast in case anyone was looking, and also because I couldn't chance her waking up and wondering what the hell was going on.

I pulled up slowly and eased the brake on so there was no sudden lurch when I stopped. Then I wrapped my arms around her and gently pulled her with me. She was lighter than I had anticipated, and I was able to manage fairly well until I got to the door which I had to unlock, and then to the steps which I had to climb. It took some juggling, and I had to prop Annie up against the side of the RV while holding the door open, but I managed to drag, carry, and heave her into the RV. I left her on the floor while I caught my breath then rolled her over and prepared to lift her to the sofa. Gripping her under her knees and neck I gave one mighty heave ho and dropped her onto the cushions. She hadn't so much as grunted. But I didn't know if I could count on that so I went looking for things to secure her with and something that I could gag her with if need be.

I removed the belts from two robes and used them to tie her ankles and wrists together after I stretched her out on the sofa. The knots were tight, but I left a lot of slack hoping she wouldn't wake up simply because she was trying to separate her limbs. Then I cut four lengths of duct tape that I could use for her mouth or anything else that became necessary should the need arise. Then I set about decamping.

I doubt I had ever done it as fast. I know I left a disorganized mess in the basement section I usually was so careful to keep clean. But because I had no water or sewer hookups nothing was that kind of "dirty." Thankfully I had already brought in the awning, which is probably the most time-consuming chore when trying to head out. The jacks came up without a hitch and I had actually brought in the step and locked the door before bringing in the slide, as Annie, who I decided I would now call Jillie, was sound asleep on the main part of it and if the noise or vibration woke her, I wanted to be a second away from being in the driver's seat and pulling out. As it was, I needn't have worried. She was snoring louder than the motor bringing in the slide.

With everything secure, I didn't bother with the mental

checklist, checking the lights or policing the site. I wasn't even going to take the cart back. I slid into the driver's seat, cranked up the engine and forced myself not to do a *Duke's of Hazard* exit.

It was one of the hardest things I had ever done, lumbering out of there, waving to people along the way, smiling and trying to distract myself from the image of hundreds of men with shotguns running behind me circling through my head. I had to keep telling myself that there was no way anyone could know yet, no way they could suspect, for the entire time it took me to leave the fairground which was probably only three miles but felt like fifty. There was still a long line of RVs backed up to check in, keeping everyone busy. No one was paying any attention to those leaving.

As soon as it was prudent, I got up to speed and made my way to the highway. I didn't really have a plan or a specific destination in mind but I felt sure I should head south. Logic said that Brick would be coming from the west, heading south if he was at all on the way, which I kind of doubted. My cell phone, and I was not even sure where it was at this point, was not beeping indicating a missed call or text. I knew Jillie's real mom and dad lived in San Francisco and if I were the mother of a child who'd been missing for over four years, I'd want her back in my arms as soon as possible. Plus, I was going to need some kind of advocate to get me out of this mess. I got on Route 126 knowing it would lead me to Route 97 heading south. From there I could go all the way to Klamath Falls where I'd been just months before. Interstate 5 would take me through California and on to San Francisco—if I made it that far. I figured two hours undetected might get me to the border, but I wasn't sure that was a good thing. Kidnapping and crossing state lines meant the F.B.I. as well as county and state law enforcement.

I had to shake my head at the wild thought that darted through it. How odd was it that in less than six months I had managed to kidnap and cart off two young girls? *What were the odds?*

A muffled snort coming from behind me alerted me to the fact that very soon I could have a confused and angry little girl on my hands. I had to put as much distance as I could between her and Robert Brynes and the posse that he was sure to amass once he discovered what I had done. Then another very odd thought occurred to me.

Would he? Would he sound the alarm, call in the Guard, have an Amber Alert issued? Could he even? Jillie wasn't his and he knew it. If he brought her abduction to the attention of the law and hence the media, surely he'd be found out. Pictures of Annie would be circulated, but even current ones would be similar to the ones circulated four years ago. And even if total strangers didn't notice the resemblance, Jillie's relatives and friends sure would. I had to smile at the dilemma I had placed him in. He was damned if he did, damned if he didn't. I wondered which way he'd go.

Then I thought of Annie's mom, and the fact that it was her birthday today. She had longed for some quiet time with a 'cuppa' tea. Today wouldn't be so quiet for her, but in the days and months to come, she would have plenty of free time, only she would be dreading it. I had to wonder again if she had been an accomplice or another victim in all this.

I looked at my gas gage as I pulled onto 97, heading south. I had enough to get to California but figured that as soon as Jillie started to show signs of waking up, I'd have to find a spot to pull over so I could explain things and either secure her further or enlist her help, depending on her attitude and whether or not she believed me about her brother, her mother, and her four-year hiatus from their lives. Plus, I had to find my phone and get in touch with Brick. He had to know I'd found Jillie; he had to start taking over this operation, call in his troops, so to speak. The last thing I needed was a shoot-out on the Interstate because I was bringing Jillie back to her rightful parents.

I had this feeling of déjà vu and had to laugh at the

absurdity of my life. I'd actually done this same thing once before, in very much the same way. Whoever said life on the road was one adventure after another, certainly knew what they were talking about! But how many times could I have the same one?

Jillie started making moaning sounds just south of Bend, by La Pine. I figured I'd better find a place to pull over and see to her.

I took advantage of a roadside pullover and stood to stretch while I stared down at Jillie, still sound asleep on the sofa.

I debated about waking her and decided that was not a good idea, so I grabbed a bottle of water from the fridge and searched for my phone. A lot of good it did me, as the screen was dark, the only message telling me there was no service. The Cascade Range was all around us, and apparently it was blocking the signal. Great!

After one more check on Jillie, I slid back behind the wheel and pulled back onto the highway. I'd been on the road almost an hour, so I knew the clock was ticking. I decided it would be a good idea to turn on the radio and listen to the news shows. It would have been a great time to have a police radio at hand; it would also have been a great time to have Brick handy, too.

Jillie woke with a scream just as we were passing a sign that said Klamath Falls, 40 miles. I was getting tired. I was on edge listening to one news show after another, and when I heard her scream I almost ran off the road. I figured it was imperative that I pull over as it soon became obvious that no matter what I hollered back to her, she wasn't going to shut up and listen. She had already managed to roll herself off the sofa and I was afraid she'd soon get out of her loose restraints and clobber me with a pan or something.

I got us safely off to the side of the road and turned back to see her on her knees using her teeth to untie the velour sash around her wrists. She was crying and sobbing and working even more feverishly when she heard me turn off the engine. I stood up and faced her. The fear in her eyes crushed me and I had to blink away tears of my own.

"Jillie, you do know your real name is Jillie, right?"

I saw a flash of recognition and she stopped gouging at her wrists. I noticed they were bleeding where she had bitten into the flesh in her haste to get free before I could pull over.

"Jillie, I am a friend of your brother's. I don't know what they told you, but Brick is alive. He's been looking for you for over four years now. And I'm trying to get in touch with him to tell him that I found you, but these damned mountains are blocking my cell phone signal." I motioned with my arm to indicate the mountain range outside the windows.

"Now I know you think Robert and Ellen Brynes are your mom and dad, and you want to get back to them, but that's just not the truth. Whether you remember it or not, they took you from your brother at a food court at a mall at Christmas time. Now I'm going to get you to the police where your real mom and dad can get involved and then you and they can decide what happens from there. I know you probably don't want to hear this, but it's all true. I am not going to hurt you. But I do need you to cooperate."

"Mom and dad aren't dead?" she whispered.

Oh dear God, these people had told her that her parents were dead, too? I tried to approach her, to wrap my arms around her, but she moved back and put her hands out to push me away.

"Your mom and dad are very much alive. And very unhappy without you."

"They died."

"No, Jillie, they didn't. These people told you that so you would be their daughter. They probably wanted you to believe they had adopted you."

"No, I knew they hadn't adopted me. I knew Snooks took me and he was mean at first, real mean. But after he got his wife back from England, he started being nice to me. He said my whole family died in a bad car wreck and now we were a family. He was my father and Ellen was my mother. I could like it and we'd get along just fine, or I could fight him and get beat and have to sleep in a dog kennel like David and Goliath."

Tears streamed down her face. "Momma, Papa . . ." The guttural, heart-wrenching sobs churning through her, causing her to slump to the floor into a tiny ball at my feet, with her hands covering her face, caused me to cry too.

I gathered her into my arms and held her as she sobbed "Momma, Momma, Momma," over and over again, and then the chorus began again with "Papa, Papa, Papa." By the time she got to Baboo, the nickname she had for Brick, I had untied her, set her on the couch and wiped her tears and made her blow her nose.

"So you're going to be good, sit in the passenger chair and not cause trouble while I take you home?"

She nodded and burrowed into my chest. I had been holding her for about half an hour now and was getting worried about our time issues. I needed to get a hold of Brick, barring that I needed to find some friendly law enforcement types before I got shot at. Because if Robert Brynes had decided to give it a go and see if I could be found quickly and Annie returned without much media fanfare, they knew exactly what I was driving—the people at The Rally had it all on file, from the color and model down to the tiniest decal, tag number and all. Sitting on the side of the road just waiting to be surrounded by overzealous do-gooders might be foolhardy.

"Okay, I know this is a very emotional time, but try to get yourself together so we can get in our seats and get back on the road. I'm thinking that if we can get south of Klamath Falls, we'll have cell reception, so we only have about 40 or 50 miles to go and then we can get this all sorted out."

"What will happen to Ellen? I love her. And today's her birthday!" The wailing began again in earnest and I had no choice but to hug her to my chest again and to croon soft reassurances to her. *Things would work out. These things take time. I'm sure Ellen could still be in her life if she wanted her to be . . .*

Finally, I set her away from me, dried her tears again and walked her to the passenger captain's chair. I belted her in, handed her a soda and a sleeve of peanut butter crackers and slid back into my seat. Then she remembered her dogs and the crying started all over again.

At Klamath Falls, I thought it prudent to fill up as I didn't know what we'd find until we got on Interstate 5. I had heard that Northern California was pretty rural in places and since I wasn't familiar with the area I pulled off the highway to fill up.

Jillie had dozed off again and was still sleeping when I pulled up to the pump and got out to pump the gas. Seventy-five dollars later, as that was all I was "allowed" without going inside, I replaced the nozzle and capped the gas tank. Walking around to check the tires, I wasn't aware of anything unusual until I was climbing back in. On the steps, my hand on the door closing and locking it, I felt something hard dig into my back, I turned and saw Jared smiling down at me.

Chapter Thirty-two

"Not a word, not a sound or you're paralyzed for life," he hissed. "Up you go."

I went up the stairs and he motioned with his hand for me to get into the driver's seat. Walking behind me, he spotted Jillie.

"Well, what have we here?"

Jillie was slumped over the armrest, leaning on the large side window, a pillow tucked under her head.

"She's just a little girl. Leave her alone. She's sleeping off the affects of Benadryl for a bee sting on her arm."

"Well, this complicates things. But as I've learned on these excursions, go with the flow. We'll just re-position Sleeping Beauty so I can have her seat." He moved toward the seat.

"Don't you touch her!" The lioness in me surprised even me.

His eyes blinked wide at the protectiveness he heard in my voice and smiled. "You'd have made a fine little mother, shame that's not going to happen now. If you don't want me mauling her, than you'd better move her yourself. Put her on the couch so I can see both of you while you drive."

"It's not safe for her to travel there without being belted

in." I wasn't going to mention that for the first hour of this trip that's where she had been, sans belt.

"Sweetheart, that's the least of your problems. Whether she even survives the next few days is going to be totally up to you. But I will tell you this, once we get to where we're going, she cannot stay with us. I have amazing plans for you and she's not included—not even as a spectator."

The gleam in his eyes was maniacal. This was a broken and desperate man, there was no telling what he had in mind this time.

"Let me just leave her here." I looked out the window. "On that bench by the window there. She hadn't seen you, doesn't even know who you are."

"I'm tempted. But I don't trust you. And I can hardly hold a gun to your back out there." He waved the gun and he was so careless with it that I thought it could easily go off.

"I swear, I'll just put her down and come back."

He looked at me, peered with bloodshot eyes into mine and sneered, "Nah. We'll take her. I figure she's leverage. There are things I might get you to do just so I won't do them to her."

His laugh was high-pitched, definitely that of a man not himself. I had to wonder why, what had set him off like this, made him sloppy in his dress, unruly in his grooming. His unshaved jaw was hinged differently, when he had laughed I had seen the glean of silver and remembered one of the twins had cracked his jawbone and it had been wired. He reeked of sour whiskey so I knew he had been drinking.

I wasn't about to argue as I suspected he was high on something else too, painkillers most likely as I knew his injuries had been severe and for all his overt manliness, he'd always been a baby about pain. He was one that alcohol and drugs made a dangerous combination for, I remembered a violent episode one Christmas when he'd taken codeine for a cough with eggnog for a late night celebration. I'd had to lock myself in our bathroom all night when he started throwing the cutlery at me. He was a bad drunk and I could only imagine alcohol and painkillers would make him a holy terror.

"Okay, I'll move her to the sofa, just put that gun away."

He stepped out of the way so I could get Jillie, tuck her arm around my neck and slide her backward, her feet dragging on the carpet, until I could get her to the sofa. I laid her down then dug behind her back for the safety belts I knew were down in the crevasse. I did the best I could buckling her in, then stood and scowled at Jared. "Where are we going?" I demanded.

"You'll know when we get there, for now just get back on 5, heading south."

I stomped up to the driver's seat, cranked the engine and pulled out, a tad faster than prudent, almost hitting a car that was backing up.

"If we hit anything, she's the first thing I'm going to take care of." He turned aimed the gun and mimicked shooting her. I immediately slowed down and focused on my driving.

"Who is she anyway? Unless I was comatose for quite a few years while I was in the hospital, she can't be the love child you had with that cop."

I debated what I should tell him. He knew who Brick was; they'd had some major altercations over the past few months and it would be just like Jared to take vengeance out on Brick's helpless little sister. If I lied about her and he found out, or if he already knew who she was, that could also spell trouble. I went for half and half. "Her name is Jillie and she was taken from her family over four years ago."

"Just like the other one, huh? What do you do, trip over these runaways?"

"They are not runaways, they were abducted."

"And suddenly it's your job to find them and return them instead of being at home taking care of me?"

"Jared, there is no more home for us. And there never will be."

My phone rang at that precise moment, and I had a good

idea who it was. It was about time he checked in, but sadly, I was not in a position to answer the phone now. Jared fished in the tote bag that was on the floor in front of the console, found the phone, slid open the window screen and holding it with two fingers, made a flourish as he dropped it. I heard it clatter against something under the RV and then saw a glimpse of it in the rearview TV monitor as it bounced and shattered on the pavement behind us.

I saw him grimace in pain from the amount of effort it took him to close the screen then the window. His injuries were varied and severe; I knew he hadn't had sufficient time to heal from them. The way he was holding his side it looked like he was still dealing with bruised or broken ribs. He saw me glancing over and shot me an angry look.

"This is all your fault! And you're going to fucking pay for it!"

There was a low moan from Jillie. Jared's harsh voice had woken her. "Wh-hat? Whatzz goin' on?"

"Jillie, we have company honey, and he's not the friendly type, so please be good and don't do anything to make him mad." I picked up the tote bag and slung it back to her. "There's crackers and some water in there. Drink as much water as you can so you don't get dehydrated."

Jared intercepted the bag and pulled it back. "Just wait a minute. I want to see what's in this before you give it to her."

"Really Jared? You think I'd give her a gun so she could shoot you for me?" I couldn't temper the sarcasm, but I should have made an attempt because I saw his face redden. He jumped up and pulled my head back by the ponytail and I screamed, "Jared, I'm driving!"

He didn't seem to care and I tried to lower my eyes just enough to catch the gray ribbon of the road ahead so I could stay on it.

"Next time you smart mouth me, I'll going to stick my cock in it. And if you do anything but suck it or lick it, I'll blow your fuckin' brains out."

As a negotiator might say, we were escalating here. And it was mostly my fault; I was not using the playbook. I had to stop ticking him off and find a way to appease him before Jillie got hurt. In my mind, it was already a given that I was going to be hurt. I needed to concentrate and do what would be best for Jillie in the long run, no matter what it might mean for me in the short run.

"I'm sorry. I shouldn't have been so sarcastic. Now let my hair go before we all get killed." That seemed to jar something in his memory for he abruptly let go and my head bounced as it snapped back with a jerk. I had to correct the over steer that caused the RV to jolt and beeline for the side of the road. Luckily, we were the only ones on this stretch of highway and I was able to pull it back safely. I was sweating big time though, for a few moments I thought it was going to roll. The odd thing was, that he hadn't seemed to really care. It was as if he had a death wish and he'd come to pick me up for the ride. Well I had news for him. I wasn't going on that one-way trip to hell with him. And neither was Jillie.

"There's nothing in the tote bag, check it out for yourself. And if you wouldn't mind, I could use some of the water, too." My new plan was to keep him occupied until I could figure out what to do. Now I was hoping Robert Brynes had manned up and had the police issue an Amber Alert. With a vehicle as high profile as this it would be a matter of just a few highway exits before some cop recognized the RV and tried to pull us over. Scratch that idea, I told myself. Jared would never let me pull over and soon we'd have cop cars chasing us all over California— just like in the movies.

Jared took a bottle of water from the bag and put it into one of the cup holders on the console and then tossed the bag back to a wild-eyed Jillie.

"Jenny, I want to go home," she whimpered. I didn't ask her which one. I'm not really sure she even knew.

"I know sweetheart, I know. Drink some water and eat something, you missed lunch, you need something on your tummy, okay?"

"I'll try," she whispered, then I heard her rummaging around in the bag. I heard her tear open the package and munch on some cheese crackers.

"Where are we going Jared, what's your plan for us. I can't drive forever, in fact, I'm beginning to get a bit tired. I've been driving all afternoon."

"Just be patient."

When we got just south of Mount Shasta, he pointed to an exit and said, "Take it."

A mile later I turned onto Route 60 heading southeast. It became apparent very quickly that we were heading into the wilderness. The road snaked and turned and there were fewer signs and less traffic. My heart sank; we were not likely to be chased down by state troopers out here. If intuition had any play in this, I was betting we were going to be roughing it, maybe even ditching the RV, boondocking at best, even with no chance of hookups sounded infinitely better. An hour later 89 became 44 and the state road meandered around until we were driving through huge thickets of trees. I had seen a sign for Lassen Volcanic national park about half an hour ago, but now, other than knowing we were heading south due to the angle of the sun, I had absolutely no idea where we were. I doubted this place was on the map.

Jared sat up, his attention now focused as he told me exactly where to turn. He instructed me to drive on the opposite side of a trail to avoid a mile of the low-hanging branches. Nearly half an hour after we'd left the main road for this one, he talked me through two tight curves and then over an earthen dam I would never have taken the Dolphin over if I hadn't been forced to.

Finally he pointed to a clearing up ahead and said, "Park."

I didn't bother with the jacks or the slide, if an opportunity came that I could get out I didn't want anything to slow me down.

Thankfully Jared didn't know enough about RVs to mention it.

"I know you have plenty of gas, but let's not use the generator. We could be here for a long time."

I sighed. Not the news I wanted to hear.

"Before it gets dark I should make something for us to eat." Maybe I could get a knife from the drawer, I thought.

"Nah, let's just order pizza," he said, and then laughed heartily.

Jillie and I didn't see the humor in it and just stared at each other, she with a dazed deer-in-the-headlights look, me with wild fury blazing in mine.

"I need to use the bathroom," I said.

"Go ahead, but don't close the door."

"You're kidding, right?"

"Nope. We're husband and wife, I've seen everything you've got."

"You haven't seen it peeing!"

"A new thrill for me," he said as he opened the refrigerator and took out a beer. The lone beer I had left from when Brick was with me. I wished I had a keg so that he could get blotto with it.

He pulled off the cap and tilted the bottle and drank down half, then gestured with the bottle for me to go ahead and use the facilities. I sneered at him as I lowered my pants and went to the bathroom. He alternated between staring at me and staring at Jillie. I hoped to God she didn't have to use the bathroom anytime soon. A man like Jared leering at her while she exposed her privates out of necessity could seriously traumatize a little girl for life. As if her life was trauma-free to this point, I thought—having been kidnapped twice, told her whole family had died, and now this nut job who I didn't doubt would seriously hurt her if she got in his way.

I wiped and flushed, then shimmied my shorts up over my hips. He didn't miss a single movement and even raised his eyebrow as if in appreciation of my performance.

"Fix some sandwiches and then we're all going to get some sleep. While I sleep you get to be tied up, and not in the way you used to like," he said with a smug leer.

"I never liked being tied up by you."

"Oh, do you like being tied up by others now?"

"What kind of sandwich do you want," I snapped.

"Something with meat."

I fixed three ham sandwiches and poured Jillie and I some milk. Jared hadn't asked for anything to drink with it and I wasn't about to offer him anything.

After he was finished eating, we were told to lie down on the bed and then he tied my hands and feet together using the clothesline he made me get from one of the basement storage compartments. Jillie got similar treatment and then he rolled us together until there was room for him beside us.

I had a gun in the nightstand, but he was on that side, and while kind enough to have tied my hands in front of me to a rope around my waist, he had tied the knots tight and looped them several times. As soon as I was sure he was asleep, I whispered words of encouragement to Jillie, and told her that her brother and his army of agents would be sure to find us very soon. I told her amusing stories about how Brick and I had met, and I told her all about Angelina, and Daniel and Julia. Then I told her about Connor and Diana. And finally she fell asleep.

It was a long time before I could get to sleep though. I was scared, worried about Jillie, and uncomfortable. Jared was snoring and grinding his teeth. I was busy trying to figure out how I could kill my husband.

Chapter Thirty-three

For two days we dry camped while Jared planned what his next move would be. He watched us continually and I know that Jillie being there was the only reason he wasn't beating me. I suspected he was thinking of ways to get rid of her and that worried me too.

I tried to find ways to keep her busy and quiet. I finally got Jared to agree to let her play games on my computer. After a heated argument he finally relented just to shut me up.

"Why would I do that?" he'd asked.

"There's no harm in it Jared, it's not like there's Wi-Fi here in the woods. We're miles from anywhere."

"And you don't have a Wi-Fi card?"

"No. I'm not even sure what that is."

It was the first and only time in my life I've lied and gotten away with it.

"Okay then. But in a few days, we're moving on and she's not coming, so get used to that idea."

I knew we couldn't stay here forever. There didn't seem to be anything on the two TV stations we were able to get about a manhunt for him, and since he didn't even know I'd stolen Jillie and could be wanted myself, there was no reason not to get on to his final destination, which he had yet to inform me of. He kept saying it was warm and sunny and we'd have everything we wanted just like at home—said he had piles of money in a secure place. I had a feeling he was talking about someplace in Mexico. Some villa in an out of the way place where I could be his "kept" woman again. And as Jillie definitely wasn't invited, I didn't want to rush him.

While he was watching the evening news, I sat next to Jillie and watched her play *Spider* for a while, then I touched her shoulder, put my fingers to my lips and turned the computer toward me. I slid the Wi-Fi card from the compartment in the computer case sitting on the table and inserted it into the slot and clicked on my email program. There were numerous messages, several from Brick. I clicked on the first one.

Jenny Darlin, where are ya? If you don't reply soon I'm going to have to come looking for you and I can tell you right now that my bosses are not too pleased with me in regard to you. They're calling you Calamity Jen. Call me. Now.

I didn't have time to answer, didn't know how I would have anyway as Jared would have heard me typing. I had just heard him yawn, stretch, and stand up. I knew I had to distract him long enough to allow Jillie to get the card back out before he saw it. We might have the chance later to email someone wherever we were. I patted her on the thigh and she nodded letting me know she understood what she was supposed to do, then I stood up and walked over to where Jared stood, the ever-ready gun in his hand.

"Can I ask you a question?"

"Fire away." He slumped down into the nook, his back against the wall, his feet hanging over the bottom edge of the bench. Out of the corner of my eye, I saw Jillie palm the card.

"Jillie, this is private, can you go in the bedroom? Is she

allowed to go in there so we can talk?"

I turned and looked at Jillie. Her eyes were wide as she took in every word. I knew she was scared, bless her heart, but she was trying not to show it. She had a lot of Brick in her. I reached back to pat her hand.

He looked at Jillie, looked over at me and simply nodded. Jillie got up and took the computer with her. He waited a few seconds and then told her to bring it back to leave it on the table. I had to bite my tongue to stifle my frustration. That had almost worked.

"So, what's the question?" he asked when Jillie was behind the closed door.

I slid into the booth opposite him stalling, and hoping he'd get the feeling of camaraderie and let his guard down. I kept hoping he'd give me some privacy in the bathroom so I'd have the opportunity to get my own gun from the nightstand drawer. If he'd only let me pull the bathroom door to. But he wouldn't. He was either paranoid or he pervertedly wanted to watch.

Until I could come up with something, I had to be civil and act interested in him and his needs without giving him any ideas. I didn't think I needed to worry about him wanting sex right now, none of us had bathed in days, and Jared was fastidious about not having sex unless we were freshly showered or at least fairly clean. For now I just needed to get him talking. "The question is: how did you find me?"

He tilted his head as if pondering what I was asking then said, "I guess it won't hurt to tell you since this is the absolute last time I'm going to need to track you down." There was an ominous sound to the glee in his voice. But I'd known from the beginning of this little jaunt that this was a make it or break it, no do-overs kind of capture. He would die with this, or I would, no one would be walking away without having sacrificed the other if we didn't end up as he wanted us—happily married again, at least to his way of thinking.

I was just praying Jillie would not be included in this game of last man standing we might end up playing. I had to find a way to get her away, I said to myself as I smiled over at him, showing avid interest in the tale of how he had managed to find me this time.

He warmed to the idea of being a storyteller and evaded the critical information as long as he could by telling me about all the trouble I had caused him, the issues with the attorneys, the business having to run without a masthead, although he did mention that all the publicity had actually helped instead of hindered sales.

"No accounting for people," I said, shaking my head. "So . . ." I prompted. "How did you track me down this time?"

"I used your cervix."

"You what?"

"You may recall that little shot I zinged you with, it knocked you out for a good while, long enough for me to take some liberties if you know what I mean . . ."

I fumed because I knew exactly what he meant. I knew as soon as I'd woken from that twilight sleep that I'd been sodomized and that my nipples had been pierced with thin gold threads inserted through some of his finest diamonds. My saving grace was that the Gateway he had designed for my labial lips was on display in one of his stores out west at the time, otherwise he'd have installed the rainbow studs made of precious gems.

But it did no good to revisit that with him now. I wanted to know how he had found me despite all my cautionary measures. "Yeah. I remember. Back to the cervix?"

"Yeah, that was brilliant on my part. I knew that if you could see or feel a piercing you'd remove it, as you'd done all the others. By the way, that ruby was worth easily $30,000, and you disposed of it as if it was costume jewelry."

"Lucky for you it had a tracing device in the setting, huh?" I couldn't help but goad him, he had treated me like shit and I had to let him know I wasn't sorry about anything. But still,

I had to temper myself and pull the reins back on my control because I needed to know what else he'd done while I'd been knocked out. "Back to your brilliant idea?"

"Yeah, it was inspired. I altered one of the ear piercing guns, the ones we use to shoot and pierce ear lobes, the one that leaves a gold stud at the same time. I made the barrel nine inches and installed a gas-propelled sleeve of studs. I filled the chamber with three studs, all with tracking devices in the hollowed out head. Of course I had to customize almost everything to get this to work, but it did. While you were in La-La Land, and naked of course—as that's how I've always preferred you—I used a speculum and inserted the barrel and fired the studs right into your cervix. Good thing I designed three, as only one embedded and attached permanently. I wanted to be sure that if you ever got away that I'd have no trouble finding you."

I was horrified, absolutely horrified. How despicable, how diabolical and evil. I vaguely remembered having some cramping when I woke that persisted for a few days, now I knew why. It was as if I was on my period, sans menses.

I knew that a woman's cervix, though numb the majority of the time responded to the slightest touch and that it could give you the sensation of having severe cramps when irritated. A fresh piercing in that sensitive tissue could have had excruciating effects if the hormones weren't pumping and keeping it soft and welcoming. Which they did when a woman was aroused, just in case a more than ample penis found its way to grazing that well-guarded porthole to the life-giving womb.

That he could have done that to me—whether he told me about it or not—certified him in my mind as demented. Any respect, love, fondness, liking of any sort, was now erased for good. I abhorred the man and had I had a gun in my hand at that exact moment, I don't doubt that I would have been able to pull the trigger and blow his head off. Either one.

"So it's still there?"

"Oh yeah."

"So why has it taken you so long to find me?"

"Well, it doesn't work as well as I had thought it would. Probably because everything had to be miniaturized to such a degree. Reception was spotty at best. I could only capture the signal if you were outside, and not surrounded by mountains. Living in this," he gestured around the interior of the RV, "didn't help. Being encased in metal blocks the signal. It took a while, because I had to plot your course in dribs and drabs. So to answer your question, I found you by using your vagina."

"You're despicable!" I deeply regretted having that man at the Radio Shack in Kansas use the scanner to detect bugs while I was down at the other end of the strip mall grocery shopping. Had I stayed with him he would have detected it on me!

"You gave me no choice. You ran away. And since you *belong* to me, I had no choice. I had to get you back. You are mine and mine you will stay."

"Even if I wanted to be with you, which I definitely do not, you're going to prison. They're going to catch you and put you in jail, there will be no more making bond, no more house arrest."

"You'll drop the charges. I'll get a slap on the wrist for the physical abuse, and I'll contribute to as many campaigns as I need to. You'll see. I'll win you back. Things will be as they were, even better. I promise."

"You shot two cops!"

"Oh yeah, well there is that. We probably should just plan on going to Mexico."

I looked at the man I had married who now was broken in body as well as spirit because of his obsession with me. "Jared, that isn't going to happen."

I thought of Brick and the intense feelings I had for him. Thinking about him and picturing us together felt so right, thoughts of him gave me peace as well as a joyful giddiness I'd never felt before, at least not like this. "I don't love you, Jared. I'm not even sure I ever did."

I knew as soon as the words left my mouth that it was the wrong thing to say. I saw devastation sweep through his expression, gut the life out of his eyes, before each feature in his face hardened and his eyes burned with fury. I knew instantly that the give and take and sharing of information was over, and that it was now being replaced with rage. I had inadvertently aroused the mad man inside him again and this time, I was going to pay for it.

He stood over me and raised his hand, brought it back in a high arch to give it power and struck me full in the face. I screamed, scrambled off the bench, and even though the whole side of my face was burning and my eye was closing in reaction to the pain, I propelled myself to the other side of the RV to the kitchen area. I managed to get my hand on the drawer and pull it open before he grabbed my hair and pulled me back. Despite the pain of him trying to drag me by my hair, I fought the harsh tug by jerking my head back and forth until I broke free of his hold. My hand, still on the drawer which had slid out with my backward movement, groped inside and made contact with a knife handle. I jerked it up, spun around and brought it down. It sunk into his shoulder and he howled. I yelled at Jillie, "Get out! Get out! Run! Run into the woods! Hurry!"

I watched him try to pull the knife out. But it was in too deep and I could see the pain was excruciating. Then as if something from inside had renewed his spirit, his face set into a steely grimace and with one powerful thrust, he jerked the knife from his upper chest. Blood spurted and soaked the whole right side of his shirt. He didn't seem affected by it. He switched the knife to his other hand and came after me. I ran for the bedroom, closing the bathroom door behind me. I didn't have time to lock it, but as I pulled the bedroom door to, I managed to get the pin in the hinge. I knew it wouldn't hold but it might give me enough time to get the gun from my nightstand. I flung myself across the bed and rolled, falling to the floor beside the bed, catching myself and landing on my feet in a squat. I pulled open the drawer, grabbed the gun and flicked the safety off. Then I stood, holding it between both hands, waiting for him to come through the door.

He didn't. I listened. I couldn't hear anything. I waited a few more seconds. He wasn't even trying to get in. Why not? *Oh Dear God, Jillie!*

He was going after Jillie. My terror was complete when I heard the front door close and the screen door slam behind it. "Jillie!"

Chapter Thirty-four

I ran around the bed, pulled the hinge pin and pushed the door open, keeping the gun raised and ready for anything. He wasn't in the RV, but I pretty much knew that already. He was going for Jillie. I ran into the living room and saw him through the windshield. His back was to me but I could tell by the way he held the knife in his hand and by his stumbling but purposeful gait that he was recovered, at least enough to give chase. I ran out the door and was a few steps behind him when he managed to catch up with Jillie who was trying to get through a thicket of bramble that had her trapped.

I could see she'd made a bad choice in running that direction, the forest was thick with undergrowth—even if she got free, he'd catch her again. He grabbed her by the arm and pulled her roughly from the bush while he raised the knife high in the air with his other arm. I fired.

I watched his back jerk upright and the hand holding Jillie's arm released her. Swaying as if top heavy, he lunged and grabbed for her again. I fired again and so did someone else. It sounded like two shots, one right after the other.

This time his body fell as if he were a marionette someone had cut the strings to. He fell to the ground and didn't move.

I turned to see who had fired. Whoever had fired at the same instant I had was off to the right partially hidden in the trees.

A man in camouflage pants with a khaki sleeveless tee spotted with sweat and torn at one shoulder stepped out from a thicket of trees. Brick. The grime on his face and the shadowy growth of beard were a silent testament to the time he'd been in the woods searching for us. But he'd come for us.

We walked toward each other and met, standing by Jared's body. Jared had been shot under his shoulder blade and in the center of his back.

"I killed him," I said.

"No. Technically, I did—double tap through the heart, back to front. You paralyzed him though. He'd've never been able to walk."

He looked up then and saw Jillie standing staring in shock, gripping a sapling for support.

"Jillie," his voice reverent in his shocked whisper.

"Baboo," her voice had its own sense of awe.

Then they were in each other's arms. He was kneeling on one knee and holding her propped between his legs, clutching her tightly to his chest and whispering, "Jillie, Jillie, Jillie," over and over again. She clasped his shoulders and sobbed as if her heart was breaking. When he finally released her to stroke her hair, caress her face and wipe her tears with his thumbs, I saw tears streaming down his face, too.

My big macho man was crying and he didn't care who saw it. It was one of the most beautiful sights I'd ever seen. It was humbling. I could sense in that moment that he knew the things that mattered most in this world, and for him, that little girl was one of them. With those tears he acknowledged that he wasn't always right, that he didn't always do the right thing, but that he would always try to fix the evil in the world if he could. I was so happy that I had helped him fix this.

He was a new man in my eyes, being able to accept help from others was a huge step away from the arrogant man who thought he knew it all. Hell, when we'd first met he thought I was a stripper. I had to smile at the memory. I heard him whispering . . . then pleading, and I knew he was begging her forgiveness.

I looked away to give them this moment, and found myself staring down at Jared, his blood pooling on the ground around his head, his face in the underbrush, the blood stain on his broad back no longer blossoming but turning dark.

I don't know what possessed me, a kind of fear I guess, but I just had to make sure. I walked over and knelt, then I turned his head using fingers threaded through his hair. His eyes were open but lifeless; I wasn't prepared for the bleak blankness or the perpetual grimace that was both shock and pain. Images of our wedding day flashed through my head—the happy couple, me laughing, young, beautiful and innocent, and him as handsome as a god, confident, superior and besotted with the woman on his arm.

I felt something heaving up inside me and I jumped up just in time to reach the bushes before my stomach turned itself inside out. Brick was beside me in seconds, holding my hair back and supporting me around the waist. I could never remember being so violently sick, for several long minutes everything churned and revolted inside me until I felt I had purged my soul. Finally, it abated, and I was able to straighten. I pulled away from Brick and ran for the RV. I had to get clean; I couldn't stand myself right now.

Running through the RV I tore my clothes off. As soon as I could jerk the shower door open and turn the shower on I stepped in, heedless of the temperature, which was quite cold. I didn't care. I was in full knowledge of the fact that I could feel the cold water and the goose bumps pebbling my skin, whereas Jared could not. Would not. Ever again. He had been my husband. I had loved him with all my heart at one time. Now I no longer did. How did these things happen, how could such a grand love diminish and then die? Was there nothing in life one could count on? When vows of eternal devotion were made, weren't they supposed to mean something? I sobbed as I reached for the soap and scrubbed every inch, soaped vigorously the skin on my arms, and dug with fevered fingers into the long strands of my hair. I was trying to cleanse my body of something, but of what, I had no idea. I hadn't gotten any of Jared's blood on me.

Tears streamed down my face while cold water pelted me and soap ran out of my mouth as I cried and shook. I was a widow now. Everything about my storybook wedding had been false, it had all gone wrong and I felt the failure deep into my core. I slumped to the bottom of the tub and hugged my knees. Then the shower door opened and I was lifted into strong, capable arms that bundled me into a thick, warm beach towel.

Brick briskly rubbed my skin to bring color back while crooning that it would be all right, that everything would get better, that I was just in shock and processing the stress of the last few days. I felt smaller, gentler hands drying my hair with another towel. I grabbed Jillie's hand and squeezed it. She brought it to her lips and kissed it. Then the sobbing began all over again, only this time for a different reason—this time because I realized that I was not a failure, that I was not a complete and utter fuck up. I had made some very special people very happy today—one of them, I was in love with. And that scared the crap out of me, because the last time I had love in my heart, I'd done a lousy job of taking care of it.

Brick was kissing the side of my neck now, and telling me to breathe, to take deep breaths, to try not to think about everything right now, to just focus on the fact that we were all alive, that Jillie was reunited with her family because of me, and that he loved me.

He picked me up where I'd been propped on his knee and carried me back to the bedroom. Jillie gave us some privacy while he dressed me in fresh jeans and a sweatshirt. Despite the heat, I was chilled. Brick told me it was a combination of the cold shower and shock and he said he wanted me dressed warmly. Then he lifted me in to his arms and carried me to the sofa where he covered me with two throws. Jillie sat on the floor by my head and brushed my hair with the touch of an angel.

Brandy was brought to my lips and I didn't hesitate, I put my fingers to the bottom of the shot glass and tipped it back until I had drained it. I took a deep breath and sighed. "I'm all right now. I was just overwhelmed. I can't believe he's dead, that I actually shot him."

"He was threatening Jillie, you had no choice. And remember, honey, he was insane, he had gone over the edge, he was not the man he used to be. His obsession broke him, destroyed your marriage and demolished everything you two had built in your relationship. You don't have anything to feel guilty about. You didn't do anything wrong, in fact you were perfect, you were smart and cunning and so unbearably brave." He kissed my forehead and stroked my arm, then gripped my hand when we heard a helicopter approaching.

"I called the local authorities and the feds are on their way. It's going to be hectic around here for a while, but I want you to let me handle everything. You and Jillie stay inside, when it's time for you both to be questioned, I'll be right here with you. Just tell the agents exactly what happened, believe me, everyone knows the situation, everyone will be understanding, most will be happier than pigs on a teat that this is all over for you."

He squeezed my hand again, smoothed the hair off my forehead with rough fingers and bent to kiss me on the lips. "Remember, when all these macho hunks start pouring in here, that you belong to me. No ifs ands or buts, you're mine." He left to join the authorities who were coming to coordinate the investigation and to sanctify the death of a prominent businessman, and to hopefully orchestrate the extraction of Jillie and me. I had managed to get this hulking RV into this remote little clearing; but no way was I going to attempt to get it out.

Chapter Thirty-five

By four o'clock that afternoon, the RV was parked in a county police parking lot, and Brick, Jillie, and I were in a helicopter making our way toward San Francisco. I had thought Brick would get Jillie and take her home, spend a few weeks settling her in and spending time with his newly-reunited family while I spent some time at a nice RV resort to regroup. But he would hear nothing of it.

"No, you're coming with me. No way am I leaving you here."

"I'm fine now Brick, really. I fell apart right after it happened, but I'm perfectly fine now, really, I am."

"That's only part of the reason I want you with me. The other is that you are the one who caused all this to happen, you found her, you managed to get her away, and you kept her safe when anyone else might have left her behind to fend for herself— instead you put her safety first. My parents are going to want to thank you. And besides, the media is all over this; you'll need someone to act as a buffer, to watch over you and see that you're safe. So you're coming with me whether you like it or not."

"If you're sure."

"I'm sure and Jillie's sure, right?" He looked over at

Jillie, who appeared pale and nervous, tucked under his arm. She had never flown before and I knew she had to be nervous about the reunion that would take place on the ground at the airport in a few minutes. She mustered a smile and said, "When you told me that my parents were alive and that Brick was, too, you can't imagine how happy that made me. I immediately loved my new mom when I met her, and dad I grew to like after a time. I was so grateful they wanted to take care of me, but I had no idea, no idea at all, that they had stolen me and then lied to keep me in line. If it weren't for you, I could have spent my whole life just living and getting by, not truly being happy because I missed my true family so very much. You can't know what a difference you've made and how unbelievably happy I am now to be going home, that I even still have a home. I'd been told for so long that every one I'd loved was gone, that I was just left behind without a thought. You can't imagine how that felt, to have lost everything all at once."

For the tenth time that day, she began crying again and was passed back to me. Brick just didn't cuddle the way a woman did when there were tears involved. Men don't embrace tears as the healing balm that they are, they fear them and just want to make them stop. And sometimes, a girl just needs one powerful, fully dehydrating bout to set her straight and make her right with the world again.

"I miss David and Goliath, will I ever see them again? And mom, I mean Ellen, what's going to happen to her?" Fresh tears welled in her eyes.

"David and Goliath?" Brick asked.

I translated for him, "David and Goliath are her dogs. Goldens that she grew up with. The Rally had a dog show she had entered them in. Ellen is Robert Byrnes wife, and although I suspect she is the reason he took Jillie, she probably doesn't know that. From what I can gather, when their own daughter died it caused marriage problems, she left him and moved back to England. He lured her back with Jillie."

Forty minutes later we were landing. Out the huge bubble that was the face of the helicopter I could see a small group of people, a man and a woman in the center were huddled together oblivious of the wind whipping their hair and clothing, their eyes anxious as they looked at the helicopter door on the side. From the woman's coloring and sharp good looks I knew she was Brick's mom, the man, light where the woman was dark, was a tall redhead, whom judging by his stylish, yet bookish spectacles, was the businessman who was Jillie's father.

As soon as the whine of the blades wound down they both came running and the entourage followed. This was a wealthy couple; it showed in their clothes, their demeanor, and the ease and familiarity they had with the aircraft. Seeing the impatience on his face, Brick handed Jillie down into her father's waiting arms. She was enveloped and held tight as he turned to share the embrace with his wife. Everyone was crying, everyone was laughing. I looked over at Brick and saw a single tear leak from his eye. Seeing me looking at him from the corner of his eye, he looked over at me and smiled, then his hand gripped my thigh and he took a deep breath. He had chased this moment for years. The guilt he had etched into his eyes had finally cleared. He had brought her home.

This day had been a long time coming and I felt like an intruder, but then Brick stood and pulled me with him and we exited the helicopter to cheers and enthusiastic waves.

I was introduced to his parents and while I would have thought they were too occupied to really pay much notice, they immediately stopped talking, handed Jillie off to Brick and embraced me heartily. I was cocooned from that moment on, not out of sight or arm's length from anyone.

We were shepherded to the waiting limo and Jillie was given the seat of honor between her parents while I was asked to sit beside her father, across from Brick. Brick had told me we'd have about an hour's drive before reaching the family estate. I was surprised that Brick came from that kind of wealth until I remembered the time he had hinted at it. He'd said his mother had remarried after his father had died, and that Jillie was his stepsister. They had been off on a cruise when Jillie had been taken. The man Brick's mother had married owned vast amounts of land that was cultivated for grape harvests. Brick had joked on the helicopter that his stepfather was to Pinot Noir what Welch's was to grape jelly.

But I was pleased with how unassuming his family was— if you discounted the limo, the ready staff, and the clothing. During the hour we were in the car I learned how down-to-earth they were. While enmeshed in the trappings of wealth, they neither flashed their advantage nor discounted it. And they shared everything they owned without quibble.

They insisted that I stay with them, that I allow them to shelter me from the media, that I treat their home as mine. I objected saying that I had a lot of things to tend to, that I'd have family coming and going as well as attorneys, chaplains, funeral planners and such. As Jared's wife, since the divorce had not progressed, I was sole heir, legal trustee, and now had a long list of jobs I had to see to or hand off. The next few weeks were going to be hell.

"Nonsense! I'll set you up in my study. George," a man whom I had been introduced to but hadn't known his title, "will act as attaché and defense against the legal eagles soon to be zooming in on you, and Shelley, here," he said, pointing to the plump and smiling women sitting across from him, "will organize everything. We'll set up the south wing with a receiving room and we have six guest quarters to accommodate your family. We wouldn't hear of you not staying and joining in on the celebration. Our Jillie is back home and you are the reason. We owe you a debt we can never repay, so you must allow us to at least try to help you out."

It did seem the perfect solution. I would need to coordinate a funeral when Jared's body was released, issue press releases for the stores, and deal with a myriad of employees. I also had all of Jared's holdings to attend to, and I was sure his attorneys as well as mine would soon be on the phone needing direction.

"Well that is very gracious of you . . ." I saw Brick's eyebrows lower in a vee as he frowned in anticipation of a negative answer, then raise and arch as he grinned when I said, "and I accept." Then he winked at me and I knew there was a good chance he'd be staying for a while too—and hopefully I might have a midnight marauder.

When we pulled through the gates and the limo glided down the long drive, I watched as beautiful gardens flashed by. It was then that I realized that I myself had enough money to live this way if I chose to do so. The thought buzzed into my head and then out again. I had no desire to live this way. I was already missing my Dolphin. I was concerned about getting it cleaned after all it had been through.

"After a few days, we'll sit down and discuss the matter of the reward, it's fairly substantial. You may want George to help set up a trust."

"Uh, Dad, you know the man who was holding Jenny and Jillie, Jenny's estranged husband?"

"Yeah? What about him?"

"He wasn't just a rich man, he was Jared Jameson."

Mr. Holton's eyes widened until his brows reached the red brown curls on his forehead. "Really? Well perhaps she would consider donating the reward to your pitifully under funded agency so you can hire more agents to assist in this kind of thing in the future. Children are not property, they should not be stolen!" He looked over at Jillie then gently unbuckled her and pulled her onto his lap. "Although they are treasures, precious treasures." He kissed her cheek and rubbed his against hers as they both leaked tears of happiness.

I handed Jillie my bottle of water and whispered, "Hydrate, hydrate, hydrate, I have a feeling you're not even close to being done with the water fall."

She smiled, took the bottle from me and took a big swig.

We all tumbled out of the limo and followed Mr. and Mrs. Holton into the front hall. The story of the fatted calf paled for this homecoming. The staff, on full alert, had prepared a feast and Jillie was welcomed back into the fold with enthusiasm. I was able to watch the interaction between her and her parents, her and the staff, and her and Brick. Her initial shyness had worn off, and everyone was giving her the space she needed to get acclimated, but I was pleased when I heard Mr. and Mrs. Holton discussing plans to bring in a professional counselor. I was worried that all their plans for her seemed to center around the estate and I was concerned that they might never let her outside the compound again. But it wasn't my place, nor was it the time to interfere in something so personal.

Brick was attentive, hardly letting her out of his sight, and that worried me too. Everyone was afraid of another abduction. The pain they had felt the day she was taken was still fresh in their minds. I sat on the perimeter, a silent assessor and found much to admire in Brick's parents. And Jillie, I was so proud of her. She was clearly made of the same stock as her brother, what a trooper she was, always with a ready smile and a quick hug for anyone arriving to welcome her back.

I excused myself around seven as I was exhausted and with the help of Shelley, I found my way to my room in the wing I had been told I could use for as long as I needed.

As soon as I saw the oversized garden tub in the enormous guest bath, I was tempted beyond bearing and immediately started taking off my clothes. While it filled I unpacked the duffle bag I had hurriedly packed when we had parked the RV, hoping I had remembered to grab my lavender bath gel. I smiled as I held it like a trophy and went back to the bathtub to generously dump a good portion of it in. Then I slid in and soaked until my bones melted and my cares dissipated with the bubbles. I had almost fallen asleep with my head back against the tiles when I heard a low knock on the bedroom door. Moments later, Brick's head poked around the bathroom door.

"A sight to warm a man's heart. And his cockles."

"What's a cockle?"

"Technically it's a shell or something puckered. Euphemistically, I'm referring to my balls. You look soft and pink and infinitely edible."

"How's the party going?"

"Winding down. Jillie was getting tired so Mom took her to get her ready for bed. I have every expectation that she will spend tonight and likely quite a few others in their bed."

"This is going to be quite a transition for her and for everyone else," I said.

"Yes, and from the other side of the fence, I've seen how difficult it can be sometimes so I'm glad my parents are taking my advice and calling in a few experts."

"Have you heard anything about the Brynes'?"

"They had already packed up and left the rally by the time the agents got there. We had a complete description of their RV and tow car and they were arrested a few hours later. It wasn't pretty; he bolted and got himself shot. She turned herself in. They were making their way to Canada. She says she didn't know how he got her, but she always suspected something wasn't right as they couldn't legally adopt her."

"What happens next?"

"They get arraigned, they go to jail, a trial date is set and then he goes to prison. They both have a lot to answer for, but at this point her culpability is in doubt. He told her he found her. She didn't know for sure that he'd taken her until you took her back."

Just then a buzzer sounded and he walked over to a console on the wall and pressed a button. "Yes Mother?"

"Figured that's where you'd gone. Jillie wants you to come say good night. Jenny too if she's available."

"She's covered in bubbles and doesn't look like she could get there under her own power right now."

There was a delightful laugh and then the button was released and it was quiet in the room. So quiet I could hear the bubbles popping all around me.

"I have to go, and if I know her, she's going to want a story." He stopped just then and stared straight ahead. I knew what he had just realized, he didn't know her, and she was past the age of wanting bedtime stories read to her. They'd lost so much time, so many years of her growing up and so many changes—Jillie wasn't a little girl anymore.

"Even though she can read now, she would probably still love for you to read to her. It's a given your mom has saved all her books and toys, find one that was special and read it to her anyway."

"Thanks." He bent and brushed his lips over mine and then with the snick of the door, he was gone.

Chapter Thirty-six

At two in the morning, I felt Brick slide into bed beside me. He had that just showered smell; a fragrant citrus and spice overlaid his all male essence and when his hair brushed my cheek as he drew me to him I could feel it was damp.

I let him draw me into his chest and entwine his legs with mine. I had found a razor and my legs were smooth. The soft hair on his legs abraded mine and I loved the masculine feel of it.

"Hi," he murmured as he kissed the shell of my ear.

"Wasn't sure you were coming back."

"Long bedtime story, even longer lecture."

"Lecture?"

"Well, not exactly a lecture. There's been this tenseness between my stepfather and me ever since Jillie went missing. An elephant in the room kind of thing. He blamed me, yet he didn't blame me. But how the hell could he not blame me? It was on my watch that she was taken, and if anyone in the world should have known better, it was I. I'd been on a task force handling just this kind of thing for seven fucking years. We had a lot to talk about. Then I had to make some phone calls. It took some time and a lot of planning, but David and Goliath are on their way here from the kennel they'd been taken to. Ellen had to agree to let Jillie have them and sign some papers to that effect, so an agent had to find her attorney and visit her at the jail she was being held in. What a long day. But that should make Jillie happy."

I leaned over and kissed him, and nodded. It would indeed make her happy.

I smelled a hint of brandy on his breath, not quite masked by his toothpaste. I sensed it might be a good time to change the subject. I was about to cry again. That was such a sweet thing that he had done.

"How did you find me?"

"What do mean, you were there—I climbed to the top of your RV and there you were sunbathing practically naked with a very large ruby in your belly button." He pulled the covers down, sat up and bent over my stomach and kissed my naked navel. The scar was long healed where the prong had fastened to the setting and pierced my flesh. His tongue was tickling me so I giggled and pushed him away and he slid back up to look into my face.

God he was so handsome, my heart lurched to know he was here, with me, and that we were both naked, warming each others skin as our legs shifted and tangled together.

"I meant this morning, how did you find me this morning." I rubbed my hand over his furred chest, tracing a firm nipple with my index finger, circling it over and over again.

"Ahh . . . well your sister called just as I was leaving Minot airport. Had this far-fetched story, but knowing it was you, I knew it had to be true. Agents were dispatched and upon arriving on the scene discovered everyone in an uproar about a missing girl. At first you weren't a suspect, then someone spoke to the people whose site was next to the Brynes'. Said they'd been furious you'd taken her, and that they were going to find you. But I guess once they realized they couldn't exactly ask the police for help, they went the other way, trying to get out of the country. Now a question for you, how did Jared manage to find you this time?"

"You're going to love this story. He pierced my cervix with one of those ear-piercing machines that he modified the night he caught me in his study and drugged me. I've got a hollow gold-studded earring with a tracing chip inside attached so far up inside my vagina that I can't feel it. It's the size of small pea and has its own tiny hearing-aid-sized battery embedded in it. With it, he was able to track me for at least a year, maybe two—however long the batteries lasted."

Brick jerked back, gripping my arms and looked into my face, "You're kidding right?"

"No. According to him it's there."

He had a thoughtful expression on his face then I saw his lips quirk.

"What?"

"I felt something when I was inside you, something I thought I nudged when I was thrusting into you once, but I thought I had imagined it."

"Hmmm . . . "

"Maybe I should check again?"

The innocent look on his face caused me to laugh. I got to laughing so hard I was crying. Then he was laughing too, and before I knew what was happening, he was on top of me, kissing me so deeply and so thoroughly that I thought he might be considering attacking this from a different angle.

An exquisite heat spread through me, and when his hand moved to cup my breast and his thumb flicked my nipple that marvelous heat streaked like an electric current to my womb. This was a dangerous, primal man who with his muscled body was pinning me to the bed and looking into my face with desperate moonlit eyes. The need and wicked smile I saw there sent pleasure racing and pulsing through me. He watched my eyes close in ecstasy and then leaning on one elbow, he bent and took the other nipple into his mouth. His teeth grazed the tip then his mouth clamped on it and tugged as the fingers of his other hand continued to pluck at my other nipple. I was dissolving, melting into the mattress with each tug. His hips meshed with mine and I felt his erection probing, invading between my thighs, retreating and evading as I squirmed to capture it back. Using his hand he pressed his erection flat against my mound then he teased with a series of forays that stroked my clit mercilessly.

With each ripple of pleasure that blazed and sent shards of lightning through me, I mumbled my displeasure with his blatant teasing, groaning each time when he delved deeper and I fought for completion. I wanted penetration of that hard, thick ridge more than I wanted anything in the world. I got penetration, but it wasn't his cock sliding into my cleft, it was his bold tongue darting into my mouth—the intensity thrilling as he built my arousal until I could no longer stand it. I had to have him inside me. Now.

Warm fingers parted my lips as he kissed me senseless, then I groaned as he pumped two fingers into my hot sheath holding his hand as if it were a gun. Each time his thumb, in the position to fan the hammer, stroked my clit and I arched and tried to crawl up his hand, shoving his fingers deeper into my core. Finally I knew what he was waiting for.

With a throttled groan I begged for release, "Brick, please . . . I need you." He thumbed his penis down until it was at my opening and with a quick jerk of his hips he plunged in and was fully seated. I was so ready I was trembling, but as soon as he was inside me I began splintering apart. My eyes flashed wide and I strangled on a scream before letting a wave of sensation wash over me. The needs tearing through me were converted into rippling, pulsing surges—an ecstasy so divine that moments later a haze of satiation sealed my eyes. I was done.

"Hey there," he whispered and I peaked up at him with one eye, "remember me?" I was so done, but apparently he was not.

"Do as you will, there's no fight left in me."

"In that case," he lifted me with a butt cheek in each

hand and hammered into me, delving deeper with each thrust as he pulled me closer. He kissed me with the kind of hunger every woman dreams about, a questing tongue scourging my mouth, and said "Fuck yes," right into my mouth. With one final thrust followed by a succession of short jabs with the power of a jackhammer he gritted his teeth and stilled as he released his semen into me. Another, "Fuck me!" and he was done. His forehead fell to the bed beside my shoulder and I could hear his labored breathing for several minutes. Then strong arms levered him up and he looked into my eyes, and whispered, "Mmmm. By passion driven, again."

"What?"

"Robert Burns, remember? The real one. You jumble up things inside me, shit you even have me quoting poetry. And by the way, yes."

"Yes what?"

"It's still there."

He fell off to the side and gathered me into his arms. After a few minutes he began stroking my cheek.

"If you can find the right radio frequency, you'll never lose me." I said. "At least until the batteries die."

"I'm tempted to do just that. It sure would come in handy. You're turning into a hard woman to hold on to."

"And you want to hold onto me?"

"More than you can imagine. More than I would have thought possible." His eyes met mine and I could see the flare of passion, the love he had for me reflected in them. My heart tripped and had to pick up the pace to get back on track.

It felt as if I had run into a brick wall. But instead of shattering when I ran full tilt into it, every cell in my body absorbed it. As if the mortar around each brick had melted, the wall that had been around Brick's heart dissolved into mine. I could feel it. I knew he was now free of his demons when his breath sighed out of him as if he had released them back into the universe. It was a cleansing sigh and it washed over me in a way that was spiritual in its intensity.

A sigh of satisfaction escaped my own lips, mesmerizing me with its reverence. This man loved me. Not in desperation or with obsession, but full of adoration and devotion for the woman he now held in his arms. Me. The look in his eyes said he was in awe of the woman staring back at him, and that while he was claiming her as his, he was also surrendering to her completely.

He pulled me on top of him and kissed me a ravenous hunger while impaling me. I gasped into his mouth. I realized we were one and that we were meant to be. It didn't get more right than this. When we came together, it was like falling from the clouds. I had to mentally pinch myself to be convinced I wasn't dreaming as his head fell beside mine and his warm lips kissed the curve of my neck. "I love you," he whispered. "Now and forever, you belong to me."

Moments or hours later, I wasn't sure which, I woke to his voice, and his fingers trailing down my arm. "By the way, I spoke to your sister, and she, along with your parents, will be here sometime tomorrow. I hope that's all right."

"I haven't seen them in ages. It will be wonderful to see them again. Are you sure your parents don't mind, I hate using their house as a hotel for my family and business interests."

"They don't want you to leave. And neither do I."

"When do you have to report back to work?"

"I took a leave of absence. I figure a week or two here with you, then a month checking off wineries in Napa. They have a wine train, with a Candlelight Inn package, even a Wedding package . . . "

That was met with silence. He didn't let it grow and become awkward, "Are you burying him in Virginia?"

"No, he'll be cremated then I'll fly back for a memorial and to finalize some business."

"Finalize?"

"I'm going to sell the franchise. I don't know the jewelry

business and I don't care to learn it."

"Well my boss says we'd make a pretty good team if you're interested in taking some training and helping out."

"That's a nice fall back, but for now, I just want to unravel. I've been running for so long, it'll be nice to just travel and not have anything to worry about, no one chasing me, no missing kids."

"Speaking of missing kids . . . have I said thank you?"

"Hmmm. Not sure. But I'm so happy you arranged for David and Goliath to be brought here. I was in the tub thinking, I'd buy her a new one. Then I asked myself why was it that every time I got a kid back to their rightful parents I ended up having to buy a puppy?"

He laughed and snuggled closer. "Well this time if you *do* get her a new one too, don't be looking for a wealthy gambler to help you pick one out, *I'll* go with you." He was referring to Craig, the man who had rescued me in Death Valley.

I kissed his neck. "He was a very nice man, and he did say he wanted to marry me."

"I said I wanted to marry you."

"You did?" I sat back and looked into his bright eyes. 'I must've missed that."

"We spoke of white picket fences and all that went along with that."

"What did I say?"

"That you needed time."

"Let me clear up my old life and then you and I can ride off into the sunset."

His lips captured mine and he took my senses away with a wickedly intimate kiss that set off those streaking hot pulses again. "I suppose you can you hook me up and get me a good price on a diamond ring when the time comes?"

I laughed, "Yes I suppose I can."

"Meanwhile, I think I'll just mosey on down and see if I can touch that stud with my tongue." He slid under the covers and tented the sheet.

I had once thought I'd had the fairy tale and then somehow screwed it up, but now I knew that wasn't true. I had never had the fairy tale until now.

Chapter Thirty-seven

I woke to sunshine streaming in the floor to ceiling windows. The drapes were pulled, but there was a gap in the middle where the sheers allowed the day to break in and share its glory.

I yawned as I attempted to turn over but Brick's arm hung around my waist like a weighted belt, with his leg thrown over my thigh I was immobilized even more. I couldn't move, I struggled to lift his arm.

"Where are you going," he whispered in my ear.

"Just trying to turn so I can face you, you've got me pinned down."

"This isn't pinned down." He rolled away, grabbed something from the nightstand and rolled back.

He snapped a handcuff around my wrist, wrapped the empty one around a wooden slat in the decorative headboard, and when that cuff was around the pole, he attached it to my other wrist, pinning me under him with my hands high above my head. "This is pinned down."

His lips grazed mine. I hadn't brushed yet so I wasn't eager for the kind of kiss he was working toward. He had other thoughts. His thumb, resting on my chin, moved to press on the corner of my mouth, forcing my lips to open for his warm, wild, searching kiss. I was being thoroughly investigated whether I wanted to be or not. He was very thorough and as he delved deeper I felt giddy.

When his arm around my waist pulled my breasts closer to his chest I felt his erection press firmly into my stomach. This was the type of arousal that could not be denied. It probed and felt along my belly for an opening. It heated my blood and jumbled my insides to know he wanted me this much, and that from all appearances, he was going to have me. I felt wicked with my arms stretched above me, vulnerable to him in every way as he kissed me senseless leaving me no option but to comply—to allow him to do whatever he wanted. It had never been this way with Jared, with him it had been fearful, not freeing.

His lips moved to my jaw and he nibbled his way to my ear. Once there, his teeth pulled on the lobe, his lips sucked it into his mouth; his tongue licked it and moved to lave the inner shell. "Mmmm . . . 'by passion driven' is my new mantra. You drive me crazy, I want you . . . so wild for you," he whispered as I groaned.

"Why do you suppose I allow you to do things to me that I wouldn't let my husband do?" I moaned as I jiggled the handcuffs—as if he didn't know what I was referring to.

"It's about trust, desire and the knowledge." He was breathing heavy against my chest, his chest hairs crinkly against my nipples and spiking them to hard points.

"The knowledge?" The confusion in my voice battled with my own panting breaths.

"The knowledge that it's all about your pleasure or it's about no one's pleasure."

"I like the sound of that, " I said, looking up into his passion-filled eyes.

He grinned down at me, "And I like the sound you make when you're reaching for an orgasm, thrusting against me, begging for a certain touch—the one special touch that will make you shatter in my arms." He kissed the tip of my nose, my eyelids . . . my lips. "I live for the scream that follows, so don't disappoint," he said as he took my lips in another tantalizing kiss."

"Don't you disappoint," I murmured against his lips.

"Oh, I assure you, I won't." His lips caressed my jaw, my neck, and then my collarbone as his fingers delved between my thighs finding me wet and ready for him. When he moved over me and entered me, I sighed my pleasure. When he pressed me into the bed as he licked and sucked on my nipples, I gasped and moaned. When he thrust and held, thrust and held, over and over again, pressing his groin into my clit and rubbing in tiny circles, I begged him not to stop. When he hit that spot, met it with the exact pressure, the exact touch I needed, I screamed as I exploded, the pleasure racing through me, splintering me. I forced my eyes to meet his, the intensity I saw forcing my own eyes to flare wide before an exquisite fog took over. I felt primal need tearing through him as he quickened his pace, pulled my legs high and anchored them with his shoulders as he shoved himself forcefully inside me. His body jerked as a prelude to his spending deep inside me. "Fuck, so good, so fucking good." His jaw clenched and a look of strained agony crossed his features. The male equivalent of a scream groaned out of him, jagged and harsh he hollered his release. He was right, it was wonderful to hear the sound of pleasure as it washed over the one you adored.

We floated and then melted into the sheets, tangled and sprawled on each other as if too intoxicated to move.

"Still there?"

"Still there. How many years do you think it will take of my penis grazing it before it wears away?"

"Well that depends. If you can get your tongue to abrade it, too . . . that might help it along."

The intercom buzzed and Brick reached over to hit a button on the console. "Yes?"

"Ask me how I knew where to find you." It was

Brick's mom.

"Now why would I be in my bed, when there's a perfectly lovely, delightfully spirited female in your guestroom who needs my company."

"Well right now I need your presence in the front hall. There's a man here with two huge crates saying you asked for them to be delivered here. And they're barking at me!"

In the background we heard Jillie's yelps of surprise, "David! Goliath!"

"Brick, you get right down here!"

He released the button and kissed my neck.

"I think we have time to go one more 'round of Go for the Gold before they send someone up."

Yes, I truly did have the fairy tale this time.

About the Authors

Jacqueline DeGroot lives in Sunset Beach, North Carolina with her husband Bill, a golf pro at Ocean Ridge Plantation. When he comes off the course and she takes a break from writing, they enjoy riding bicycles, walking on the beach, lounging at the pool, and making plans to take off in their "vintage" RV. She loves to hear from readers and has a website you can visit at *www.jacquelinedegroot.com*

Peggy Grich, along with her husband Jim, are full-time RVers. She has edited and published over 20 books. Peggy and her husband produce *American RVer*, a monthly Internet-based Television Show for RVers, featuring their RV travels, technical tips, and interviews with friends they have met across America. It can be seen at *www.americanrver.com.*

CPSIA information can be obtained at www.ICGtesting.com
Printed in the USA
BVOW04s0850060916

461057BV00001B/9/P